Do you need a cowboy fix?

New York Times *bestselling author*
Vicki Lewis Thompson
returns to Harlequin Blaze in 2012

with more...

Sons of Chance

Chance isn't just the last name of these rugged
Wyoming cowboys—it's their motto too!

Saddle up with

#687 Long Road Home
(June 2012)

#693 Lead Me Home
(July 2012)

#699 Feels Like Home
(August 2012)

And don't forget about the ebook prequel,

Already Home

(Available in May 2012)

Take a chance...on a Chance!

P9-ELR-303

Blaze

Dear Reader,

Have you ever wanted desperately to connect with someone, yet not known for certain whether they'd accept you? That's the uncomfortable position in which Wyatt Locke finds himself as he drives toward the Last Chance Ranch in the first Sons of Chance book of the summer. Yes, folks, Wyatt's story kicks off another three-book parade of gorgeous cowboys!

Although Wyatt longs to be friends with his half brother Jack Chance, he's so afraid of rejection that he doesn't notify Jack that he's coming. That plan doesn't work out as he expects, but in Wyatt's shoes, I would do the same.

In writing about Wyatt, I longed to protect him from getting hurt, so I gave him Olivia Sedgewick, someone who sympathizes with his desire to connect with family. But even Olivia can't stand between Wyatt and disappointment. As it turns out, getting hurt and learning from the experience is how people grow.

And just so you know, Wyatt doesn't start out the story as a cowboy, but before long, he's wearing the jeans, the boots and the hat. They're borrowed, but they do the trick. Taking yummy-looking guys and turning them into yummy-looking cowboys is what I do.

Welcome back to the Last Chance Ranch, and thank you for joining me there once again! It's been a long winter, but now that summer is finally here, my cowboys are saddled up and ready to ride straight into your heart!

Warmly,

Vicki Lewis Thompson

Vicki Lewis Thompson

LONG ROAD HOME

TORONTO NEW YORK LONDON
AMSTERDAM PARIS SYDNEY HAMBURG
STOCKHOLM ATHENS TOKYO MILAN MADRID
PRAGUE WARSAW BUDAPEST AUCKLAND

PLEASE RECYCLE · THIS PRODUCT IS RECYCLABLE ·

Recycling programs
for this product may
not exist in your area.

ISBN-13: 978-0-373-79691-5

LONG ROAD HOME

Copyright © 2012 by Vicki Lewis Thompson

ABOUT THE AUTHOR

New York Times bestselling author Vicki Lewis Thompson's love affair with cowboys started with the Lone Ranger, continued through Maverick and took a turn south of the border with Zorro. She views cowboys as the Western version of knights in shining armor—rugged men who value honor, honesty and hard work. Fortunately for her, she lives in the Arizona desert, where broad-shouldered, lean-hipped cowboys abound. Blessed with such an abundance of inspiration, she only hopes that she can do them justice. Visit her website at www.vickilewisthompson.com.

Books by Vicki Lewis Thompson

HARLEQUIN BLAZE

*Sons of Chance

To get the inside scoop on Harlequin Blaze and its talented writers, be sure to check out blazeauthors.com.

All backlist available in ebook. Don't miss any of our special offers. Write to us at the following address for information on our newest releases.

Harlequin Reader Service
U.S.: 3010 Walden Ave., P.O. Box 1325, Buffalo, NY 14269
Canadian: P.O. Box 609, Fort Erie, Ont. L2A 5X3

To my wonderful readers, especially those of you who've been with me from the early days. Your emails and letters mean the world to me!

Prologue

August 22, 1978
From the diary of Eleanor Chance

JONATHAN IS MARRIED, and my heart is heavy. We had a small ceremony this afternoon at the Last Chance because that's all he and Diana wanted. There's no pretty way to say this—a baby is on the way, and after several months of debate, Jonathan and Diana decided to get married. If you're in love, you don't debate such things, so I've concluded they're not in love and I hate that for both of them.

Oh, they say they love each other, but I think that's so Archie and I won't be upset about this marriage. Jonathan is our only child, and of course we wanted him to end up with a woman he adores, who also adores him. We hoped she'd share his devotion to the ranch and look forward to raising children here. Our grandchildren.

Instead he has Diana. She looks like an Indian princess, which makes sense because her mother was Shoshone. Other than that, she hasn't volunteered much about her parents except to say they're both gone.

I have to wonder what her upbringing was like, because she's the least nurturing person I've ever come across. She pretends to be happy about the baby, but I can tell she's not.

She confessed to me that before she found out about her pregnancy, she'd been saving her tips from waitressing to finance a move from the Jackson Hole area to San Francisco. She'd dreamed of getting out of Shoshone, which she calls a one-horse town, and living a more sophisticated life.

Instead she's stuck here, and I can tell that's exactly how she feels, too. I seriously doubt she looks forward to living on the ranch for all her born days, and if she stays with Jonathan, that's what she'll have to do.

I'm torn because I don't think the marriage is a good idea, but she's carrying my grandchild. For that reason, I want her to stay right here and learn to love being a mother to my grandbaby and a wife to my son. I plan to do everything in my power to help that cause.

1

If Wyatt Locke believed in omens, his return visit to the Last Chance Ranch had disaster written all over it. Rain drummed on the roof of his truck and sluiced over the windshield faster than the wipers could sweep it away. Every so often lightning would strike close enough to deafen him while providing a camera-flash view of the muddy road and the soggy Wyoming countryside.

The storm had come on quickly, ambushing him after he'd already committed to the rutted dirt road leading to the ranch. The weight of his camper shell and the gear in the back helped keep him on the road, but trying to turn around now would almost guarantee he'd end up axle-deep in mud. Going forward was his only option.

He slowed the truck to a crawl and kept his headlights on, although they didn't accomplish much. Still, he'd hate to run into something. A pair of taillights winked in the distance to let him know he wasn't the only fool out here. But then the rain got serious again and reduced visibility to about fifteen feet in front of him.

If his twin brother, Rafe, could see him struggling through this deluge, he'd laugh himself silly. Rafe had tried his best to talk Wyatt out of this harebrained scheme, but once Wyatt latched on to an idea, he couldn't let it go. Jack Chance was his half brother, damn it, and they should get to know each other. Jack was Rafe's half brother, too, but Rafe wasn't interested in cementing any family ties.

The rain let up for a second and there were the taillights again, several yards in front of him. Probably one of the ranch hands coming back from town. Could even be Jack.

Wyatt's gut tightened as he thought about his half brother. He probably should have alerted Jack that he was coming, but he knew exactly why he hadn't. He'd been afraid Jack would tell him to stay away.

Wyatt had shocked the hell out of him the previous summer by dropping by the ranch to introduce himself. He'd shown up without warning that time, too, not sure until he'd knocked on the ranch house door that he'd go through with it. Realistically, he should have expected Jack's chilly response.

No doubt Jack hadn't believed him at first. He would have believed Rafe right away because the two men looked so much alike, both having inherited their mother's dark hair and eyes. But Wyatt and Rafe were fraternal as opposed to identical twins, and Wyatt had ended up with his dad's sandy hair and gray eyes.

Eventually Jack had seemed to accept that Wyatt was his half brother, but he'd remained suspicious, as if Wyatt might want to cash in on the financial success of the Paint horse breeding operation at the Last Chance. No, and hell no. Wyatt had a profitable wilderness trekking company based in San Francisco and wasn't the least bit interested in Chance money, but Jack couldn't know that.

The money issue wasn't the biggest reason for Jack to be prickly, though. Finding out that the mother who'd abandoned him had subsequently married a successful businessman and raised two more kids couldn't be an easy pill to swallow. Worse yet, she'd kept Jack's existence a secret from her second family until last year when the divorce from Wyatt and Rafe's father had apparently loosened her tongue.

Hiding the fact she'd had a kid thirty-odd years ago was pretty radical, even for his mother. But it wasn't totally out of character. Diana had always been evasive about her past, as if she was ashamed of it. She claimed that she'd been through hard times and nothing more needed to be said. Yeah, well, she'd put Wyatt and Rafe through some hard times as they tried to deal with a completely self-absorbed mother.

The taillights disappeared again as the rain redoubled its effort to drown this part of the country. Wyatt had years of experience handling every kind of weather, and he'd be damned if he'd end up in a ditch this afternoon and have to call the ranch for help. That wouldn't improve his rep any.

And he wanted his rep to be solid, wanted Jack and everyone else on the ranch to think of him as a competent outdoorsman, even if he wasn't a cowboy. Maybe he and Jack would have things in common other than the obvious connection of having the same mother. Wyatt liked the idea of being related to a rancher.

He'd always felt out of place in the circles his parents preferred. Rafe, with his business degree and his talent for investing, fit right in. Not Wyatt. He'd taken up hiking and camping as a teenager to escape charity balls and gallery openings.

Jackson Hole had some of that high society element going on, especially within the Jackson city limits. But the little town of Shoshone about ten miles from the ranch was definitely more Wyatt's style. A collection of small businesses and a single traffic light at the only major intersection—that was urban enough for Wyatt.

If he chose to, he could relocate his company here. Adventure Trekking could operate as well—or maybe even better—from the Jackson Hole area as it did out of San Francisco. If he lived here, he could spend time at the ranch and get to know the Chance family. He had a feeling he'd fit in with them better than he ever had with his own family.

But before he made any drastic changes, he needed to find out if Jack had mellowed toward the idea of Wyatt's and Rafe's existence. Jack's resentment could be a major obstacle to Wyatt's plan. The guy had obviously been hurt when Diana had left him, but in Wyatt's opinion, Jack might have been better off without her in his life. Wyatt had asked around town, and the guy seemed to be doing just fine.

Sure, his father had died a while back, but he still had his stepmother, Sarah, and two half brothers, Nick and Gabe. They all owned a part of the ranch and, according to what Wyatt had heard, everyone got along great. Jack was happily married now and had a kid of his own.

Wyatt planned to keep that last bit of info to himself. He wasn't sure how Diana would react to finding out she was a grandmother, and Jack didn't need to have her suddenly appear and claim her grandmotherly rights. She might not care a whole lot about the baby, but she loved being the center of a drama.

If Jack had a baby, that made Wyatt an uncle. He smiled at the idea. It was kind of cool to think about. Maybe he should have brought something for the baby, especially because he was once again arriving unannounced. But he hadn't....

Lightning flashed, nearly blinding him with its intensity. For a split second the road was lit up like a movie set. A crack of thunder followed, loud enough to make his ears ring. But in that brief moment of full light, he'd seen a Jeep Cherokee off on the side of the road up ahead, its right wheels buried in mud, the taillights still on.

He hadn't been able to tell if the vehicle was occupied, but he guessed it was if the lights were on. Once he was alongside it, he stopped and lowered his passenger side window to get a better look.

The driver's window on the Jeep slid down, too, which gave him his answer even before he saw the pretty woman with the hopeful expression gazing over at him. Her shoulder-length hair was streaked with red and blond, obviously a salon job and not her natural color, but it looked good on her. The Cherokee's taillights must have been the ones he'd followed down the road.

"Seems like you're stuck!" he called out over the sound of the rain.

"Yep! I was about to phone the ranch. Maybe somebody can come get me."

"I'm headed that way, if you want a ride." He knew what he was suggesting wasn't a perfect solution. That salon hairdo would be dripping with water by the time she made it into his truck, and her shoes would be covered with mud. But she'd be in the same fix if someone drove out here to get her. Trying to hitch a tow chain to her Jeep in this downpour with lightning flashing all around wasn't reasonable.

A couple of seconds went by with rain coming in his open window and hers, too, probably. He had a chance to study her a little, which added to his initial impression that she was pretty—high cheekbones, rounded chin, full lips and very blue eyes. He wondered if she was worried about accepting a ride from a stranger. "My name's Wyatt Locke," he said. "I'm Jack Chance's half brother visiting from San Francisco."

"Sarah didn't mention anyone coming to visit today."

Wyatt wondered if Jack's stepmother would be annoyed because he was dropping in. "It's a surprise. But if you want to call the ranch and double-check that I'm legit, go ahead. The surprise isn't that important." And they couldn't tell him to leave with this gully-washer in progress, even if they wanted to.

She smiled, revealing even white teeth with a tiny space in the middle. "I'm sure you're perfectly safe, Wyatt Locke. Serial killers don't usually come out in weather like this." She glanced at the seat next to her before turning back to him. "But I have a couple of bags of stuff I need to take up to the ranch house."

"Will it get ruined if it gets a little wet?"

"Not really, but—"

"You can't carry it all in one trip," he said, making a guess.

"Right."

"Hang on. I'll help." Leaving the motor running, he opened his door and stepped out. He was drenched immediately. Cold water soaked his Adventure Trekking T-shirt and hiking shorts, and burrowed into his hiking boots.

"Wait!" she called out. "You don't have to—"

"Yeah, I do. Can't leave a damsel in distress." He slogged around the front of the truck, his boots making a sucking sound with every step. First he opened his passenger door and then turned toward her Jeep. "Let's get your bags in there first. Do you have an umbrella?"

"No such luck." She opened her door and passed him two large zippered totes.

"Got 'em." Water ran in rivulets down his face, but now that her door was open he could see the rest of her if he blinked the rain away. She had a great figure, nicely showcased by jeans and a black scoop-necked top. Then he noticed her feet. Dear God, was she wearing high heels? Not good. "Stay put. I'll come back for you."

"No need. I'll take off my shoes and roll up my pant legs for the trip over."

"It'll be better if I carry you," he called over his shoulder as he navigated the short but muddy stretch between her Jeep and his truck. He put the totes on the floor of the cab and turned back to her.

She had one bare foot propped on the edge of the seat as she rolled her pant leg up and her toes had some sort of glittery stuff on them. Her left arm and leg were already wet from the rain coming in the open door.

"You really don't want to step out here. It's nasty."

"It's only mud." She glanced up at him, her blue gaze resolute. "You can go back to your truck. I'll be right there."

"But I'm already a mess. If I carry you over, you won't have to be."

She looked him up and down. "Yes, but the footing is terrible. You could easily slip, and then where would we be?"

He swiped the rain away from his eyes. "I won't slip." By now his boots were so full of water they'd keep him well-stabilized.

"I'm sure you wouldn't *mean* to slip, but how often do you carry a person who weighs a hundred and... twenty through the mud?"

He couldn't help grinning. Women and their weight issues. "More often than you'd suppose. I'm a wilderness guide, and I'm certified for search and rescue. In other words, I'm a professional."

"Oh. That explains the Adventure Trekking logo on your truck and your shirt."

"Exactly. I could carry you even if you weighed one-thirty." He was guessing at how much she'd subtracted from her actual weight.

Her cheeks turned pink and her chin lifted. "One-twenty-six."

She wore it well, too. "Come on. Just let me do my thing. It would be a shame to get those sparkly toes all covered with muck."

"They'd wash off, but…all right, Wyatt Locke of Adventure Trekking. You're getting soaked, and you've convinced me I'm just being stubborn."

"I wasn't going to say that."

"I believe you, and that kind of restraint is impressive." She smiled at him. "Let me put my shoes in my purse before you hoist me out of here."

He waited as the rain plastered his clothes to his body. He hadn't been this wet fully clothed since the time he'd fallen in the Snake River on a canoe trip two years ago.

"Ready." She hung her purse strap around her neck and scooted out from behind the wheel. "Can you get the door once I'm out?"

"Uh-huh." Moving into a half crouch, he slid one arm under her knees and the other behind her shoulder blades. She felt warm, soft and infinitely huggable. If it were up to him, she wouldn't lose an ounce of that one-twenty-six. "Put your arms around my neck."

She did, bringing with her a tantalizing scent of jasmine.

He was starting to enjoy himself. "On the count of three. One, two, *three*." He lifted her, taking care not to bang her head on the door frame, and stood slowly as she nestled against him. "Okay?"

"Yes."

He was more than okay. Coming to the aid of a beautiful woman—he'd upgraded her from pretty to beautiful—was a rewarding experience. Besides getting points for gallantry, he was required to cuddle with said woman for a brief time, all in the name of a heroic rescue. He turned toward his truck.

"Don't forget the door."

"Right." Which he had. The sensual pleasure of holding her had short-circuited his brain.

Rotating in place, he nudged the door with his left knee. The sideways tilt of the Jeep meant gravity was in his favor, and the door swung closed with a solid clunk. But using his knee to close the door threw him slightly off balance.

She let out a little cry of alarm and tightened her hold on his neck. "Don't you dare drop me!"

"Easy does it. We're fine." He regained his balance and adjusted his hold. God, she felt good in his arms. Part of that was her welcome warmth against his chilled body, but he could get that from a hot water bottle. She was a lot more satisfying to hold, and he was reminded that he'd been so busy working in the past year or so that he'd abandoned his social life.

The trip to his truck took maybe five seconds, and he cherished every one. Too soon he had to lean down and slide her onto the fabric seat, which was also wet after having the door open so long. "There you go."

"Thank you." She scrambled onto the seat and unhooked her purse from around her neck. He thought she'd go for her shoes, but instead she put the purse on the floor with the bags and started running her fingers up through her wet hair as if trying to save the look she'd started out with.

Shrugging, he closed the door and sloshed around to the driver's side. A woman's concern with her appearance was usually a warning signal for him after all the years he'd spent watching his mother obsess about her hair, makeup and clothes. But he didn't know this particular woman well enough to make snap judgments.

Hell, he didn't even know her name. Climbing into the truck, he closed the door and fastened his seat belt. She was still futzing with her hair. "It looks fine," he said.

She laughed and finger-combed it back from her face. "I'm sure it doesn't, but thanks for saying that. I'm Olivia, by the way. Olivia Sedgewick. And I appreciate you rescuing me and keeping my feet clean."

"You're welcome, Olivia. Nice to meet you." And he meant it sincerely. He flashed her a smile for added emphasis.

"The thing is, I'm a beautician, so I like to arrive at an appointment somewhat pulled together."

"You have an appointment at the ranch?" He put the truck in gear, and after a moment's hesitation while the tires worked out of the mud, it moved forward.

"Uh-huh." She took her trendy heels out of her purse and slipped them on her feet. "Sarah hired me to come out and give everyone manicures."

"Everyone?" Wyatt had only spent about ten minutes with Jack, but he couldn't picture the guy getting his nails done.

"All the women, I mean. Most of the guys are out of town this weekend at a horse show and sale, so Sarah decided to schedule a night of beauty for herself and her daughters-in-law, plus a few other women connected to the ranch in one way or another. I'm going to try and get a few pedicures in there, too."

"Oh." Wyatt wished to hell he'd pushed past his fear of rejection and called ahead. "I assume that means Jack's gone, too."

"I'm afraid so." She glanced at him. "Sorry. Kind of messes up your surprise, doesn't it?"

"It kind of does." He stared out the windshield. Maybe the storm had been an omen after all. Not only had he missed Jack, he'd landed in the middle of a girls-only beauty shindig. He had bad timing all the way around.

2

OLIVIA FELT SORRY FOR her hero. Wyatt Locke seemed like a really nice guy, besides being serious eye candy. His wet T-shirt clung to muscled pecs and washboard abs that made her little heart go pitty-pat.

The trip from her Jeep to his truck had been a true delight. She couldn't remember the last time she'd been carried, let alone by a guy with such a hard body. On top of that, he had nice eyes, a great smile and he hadn't dropped her in the mud.

But now, after his outstanding rescue, he wouldn't get to spring his surprise on his half brother, at least not immediately. She tried to come up with a consoling statement. "Jack can still be surprised when he comes home tomorrow night."

"I guess. But once the weather clears up, I'll head back to the Bunk and Grub for tonight."

Although the Bunk and Grub B and B wasn't far away, she was still surprised he had a reservation there. "You weren't planning to stay at the ranch?"

"Uh, no."

"But I thought you said you were Jack's half brother."

"Yeah, well." He sighed. "It's complicated."

Olivia was beginning to understand the Chance family was full of complications. Although she'd only arrived in Shoshone from Pittsburgh last fall, her job in the local salon, To Dye For, guaranteed that she heard all the gossip.

Within a couple of months she'd found out that each of the Chance men had a different mother. Jack's mom had left when he was two, Nick had been the result of a brief affair and Gabe was the only biological son of Sarah, Jonathan Chance's second wife and now his widow. But according to everyone in town, Sarah treated all three as her own.

Now here came another half brother, but he'd only made reference to Jack. "This is really none of my business," she said, "so you don't have to answer, but I'm curious as to how you and Jack are related."

"We have the same mother."

"Ah." So that was the much-maligned Diana who'd taken off all those years ago. Any time her name was mentioned, people made a face. "And is she…"

"Alive and well in San Francisco."

"Hmm. I take it she and Jack aren't close?"

"They've had no contact since she left the ranch."

Olivia considered that for a moment, trying to imagine such a thing. Nope, couldn't do it. "But you're here now."

Wyatt heaved another sigh and stretched his arms against the steering wheel. "I didn't find out Jack existed until last summer, and I…I'd like to get to know the guy."

"She kept Jack a secret?"

"Yep."

Olivia didn't say what she thought about that because Diana was his mother, after all, but apparently the people who made a face at the mention of her name had good reason. "Does Jack know you exist?"

"Yeah, because I paid him a short visit last August. We left the situation sort of open-ended. I decided to come back and see…"

The longing in his voice made her heart ache. "Are you an only child?"

"No. I have a twin brother named Rafe." He paused. "He thinks coming here is a dumb idea. And maybe it is."

"No, it's not a dumb idea," she said softly. "I don't have any brothers or sisters, but if I suddenly found out I had one tucked away somewhere, I'd be making tracks for wherever that person lived. I mean, they're your blood. That has to count for something."

He sent her a look of gratitude. "I think so."

Rain continued to pound the roof of the cab and splash against the windows, cocooning them from the rest of the world. A sense of intimacy enhanced by his impressive rescue almost made her comfortable enough to touch his arm in a gesture of understanding. Almost.

"You said you don't have brothers or sisters, so you must be an only child," Wyatt said after a moment of cozy silence.

"I am. My mom died soon after I was born, and my dad never remarried."

"Were you lonely?"

Yes, achingly lonely. But she gave him the answer

she always gave. "Not really. My dad's an inventor so he worked at home. He kept me company."

"An *inventor*." Wyatt sounded impressed. "You don't hear that every day. Has he invented anything I'd know about?"

"Actually he came up with a razor blade that never wears out."

Wyatt gave a low whistle of surprise. "Is it available? Because I would buy that in a second. I have to shave twice a day."

That comment directed her attention to his strong jaw. He must have shaved recently because no stubble showed, and now that he'd mentioned shaving, she remembered that she'd noticed a mint scent when he'd carried her to his truck. "Sorry, but the blade's not available."

"When's it coming out?"

"It's not. One of the big companies, and I'm not allowed to say which one, bought the patent because they didn't want that product on the market. They said it would wreck their profit margin."

"Damn. Can I just buy one from your dad?"

"'Fraid not. He had to destroy everything, including his research notes, in order to get the payoff. But it was a lot of money. That's why we're here, actually. He always wanted to live in Jackson Hole, so once he had the means, we pulled up stakes and left Pittsburgh."

"You live with him?"

Olivia shook her head. "God, no. I had to deal with his cluttered lifestyle when I was a kid, but I don't have to now. I live nearby so I can keep an eye on him and make sure that he eats, but I have my own place."

"He sounds like an interesting guy."

"Interesting, maddening, funny. He looks like that picture you've probably seen of Albert Einstein, white hair sticking out everywhere."

"Really?" He glanced at her. "But Einstein was old in that picture. You can't be much over twenty-five."

"I'm twenty-eight, and Dad was fifty when I was born. His hair was already turning white then, and now it's a hot mess. Besides being a nail tech I also do hair, but he won't let me give him a decent haircut. He'd rather cut it himself with my mother's old sewing scissors."

"At least he's not vain."

That made her laugh. "No, he certainly isn't. I've tried telling him how handsome he'd look if I trimmed his hair, and he just shrugs and says he doesn't care about that."

"Speaking of your work, I really don't see myself hanging around during a night of beauty."

"Maybe not, but I don't think Sarah's going to stand for you staying at the Bunk and Grub, either. It's a very nice B and B and it's almost like being with family because of Pam's connection, but still, Sarah's going to want you here, I'll bet." From what Olivia knew of the woman, she was virtually sure of it. A long-lost half brother wanting to connect with kin would touch Sarah's heartstrings.

"Pam Mulholland is part of the Chance family?"

"You didn't know that?"

Wyatt shook his head. "There's probably a lot I don't know. And I want to."

"She's Nick Chance's aunt, his late mother's older

sister. In fact, Pam will be at this thing tonight, assuming she made it over before the storm hit."

"She probably did. Somebody else checked me in this afternoon and said Pam would be gone overnight."

"Pam didn't recognize your name when you made a reservation?"

"She didn't act like she did. Jack and Sarah are the only people I met when I came here last August. Maybe they decided to keep my visit quiet."

"Maybe." Although intimate details of people's lives were freely bandied about in Shoshone, Olivia figured the town had its share of secrets, too. Wyatt might be one of them. "I'm guessing you didn't leave a phone number or an address with Jack."

"No. To be honest, he was so abrupt that I wasn't sure I'd come back. I understand why he might not welcome me with open arms, but like you said, we're blood. I'd hate to miss out on…well, friendship, at the very least, and a deeper connection if such a thing is possible. Rafe doesn't hold out much hope and doesn't seem to care whether Jack accepts us or not. But I…I do."

Olivia turned to him. "I like your courage and persistence, Wyatt Locke. I'm glad you decided to come back and give the brother deal another try, because it means we got to meet."

He grinned at her. "Same here, Olivia. But no matter how much I like you, and I do, I'm still not up for a night of beauty with the girls."

DESPITE THE DIFFICULTY he'd had driving through the storm, Wyatt was sorry when they reached the circular drive in front of the two-story log ranch house. He felt that he and Olivia had made a connection during that drive, and now that it was over, he wasn't sure how to keep it.

He really did plan to head back to the Bunk and Grub the minute the storm passed. There would be no advantage in hanging around. Olivia would be busy doing her job and he just didn't fit in with an evening of foot massages and nail polish. Maybe he'd drive into town and get a beer and a burger at the Spirits and Spurs, Shoshone's local bar.

Several trucks and a couple of SUVs were parked to the left of the ranch house. "A lot of people are here," he said. "Who did you say was coming?"

"Well, there's Pam, as I mentioned, and Mary Lou, the ranch cook, and Sarah's three daughters-in-law—Dominique, Morgan and Josie. They each have homes on the ranch, but it's not really walking distance so I'm sure they drove in. Then Morgan's sister Tyler will be there—she's married to Josie's brother Alex."

"Everybody's sort of connected, aren't they?" It sounded nice to Wyatt. Really nice.

"It's a close-knit group. Oh, and I'm pretty sure Emily will be there. She's the daughter of the ranch's foreman, Emmett Sterling, and she married Clay Whittaker this past spring. He runs the stud program at the ranch. I did everybody's nails for that wedding. Great party."

As Wyatt had suspected, this was exactly the kind of family he'd always longed for and never had—informal and good-hearted. But they might not let him in. He quickly shoved away that thought, which was way too depressing to contemplate.

The house itself looked as massive as he remembered. The barn, corrals and other outbuildings were located down the hill to the right, and were nearly obscured this afternoon by a heavy curtain of rain.

Over the winter months, Wyatt had pried some information out of his mother about the place. When she'd moved in as a bride, the house had a two-story center section plus a wing on the right, a wide front porch running the length of the house and a circular driveway. The two medium-sized spruce trees she'd mentioned being located in the middle of the circle now stood at least thirty feet tall.

After Jack was born the family had added the wing on the left and extended the porch. On each side porch a row of rockers, shiny with rain, moved gently in the wind. Rain had flattened the plants in the flower beds on either side of the wide front steps, and water gushed from downspouts to puddle in the gravel driveway.

Both wings were set at an angle like arms flung open in welcome, and lights glowed from the windows on this stormy afternoon, inviting travelers inside. Wyatt figured some travelers were more welcome than others. And his category was still in question.

Olivia looked over at him. "I don't think it's going to let up. We'll have to make a run for it."

"You're right." Wyatt wondered if he could get away with dropping her off and heading back down the road. Not likely. That would force her into breaking the news that he was here and he'd look like a damned coward for leaving. "Let me pull up closer to the steps. Then you can unload without having to walk on that sloppy gravel in your nice shoes, and I'll move the truck once you have everything out."

"Believe me, I'm regretting the shoe decision, but at the time I was going for stylish."

"They are that." He put the truck in Reverse, backed up a ways and cut the wheel. Then he pulled forward and edged right up next to the steps.

"But if I'd worn sensible boots, you wouldn't have had to haul me over to your truck." She picked up her purse and one of the two bags.

"I enjoyed it."

She gave him a quick smile. "Me, too."

That comment made him bolder. "Listen, I'm not sure how this visit will turn out for me, but can I give you a call before I leave town?"

"Sure." She zipped open her purse, rummaged around in it and came up with a business card. "My cell's on there."

"Thanks." He took the pink card, which advertised the beauty salon, To Dye For, but also gave Olivia's name and number. "I've toyed with the idea of relocating here."

"Really?" Her gaze met his. "That would be nice."

"Meeting you gives me some extra incentive."

Her blue eyes warmed. "Good."

He had the craziest urge to kiss her, but it was too soon, and he didn't want to ruin everything by overstepping.

Then, to his amazement, she leaned toward him and quickly brushed her lips against his. "Thanks for rescuing me today." She pulled right back, as if to signal it was a one-time shot.

The kiss came and went so fast he didn't have time to close his eyes, much less reach for her. "You're welcome." His voice sounded a little rusty, which wasn't surprising since he was busy processing the soft feel of her mouth.

"I'll come back for the second bag in a sec." She opened the door and let in a gust of wind and rain. "Man, it's some storm!"

"Yep." Wyatt watched as she navigated the rain-soaked steps to deposit her purse and the first bag beside the door. As far as he was concerned, it was a wonderful storm. Without it, he would have arrived at the ranch, discovered Jack wasn't there, and driven back to either the Bunk and Grub or the bar. He might have met Olivia in passing but they wouldn't have talked, not when she was there to create nail magic.

Instead they were well on their way to becoming friends. Wyatt was really starting to like it here. The country was beautiful, even in the rain, and the local residents, including a certain blue-eyed beautician, interested him a great deal.

Leaning back in, she grabbed the second bag. "Okay, that does it. I'll meet you inside."

"Right."

She paused, and her eyes narrowed. "You *are* coming inside, aren't you?"

"Yes, I am, but I'll leave my muddy boots on the porch. I actually considered asking you to make my excuses, but I didn't think you'd appreciate that."

"Good guess. And besides, you don't want to miss the food."

Wyatt imagined finger sandwiches and tea cakes

washed down with wine coolers. "That's okay. Once the storm lets up, I'll go into town and—"

"No, really. You don't want to miss the food. See you inside." She started to close the door but opened it again. "Can I say that you're here? Or do you want to make a grand entrance?"

He chuckled. "Do I strike you as a grand entrance kind of guy?"

"No, but you did mention this was supposed to be a surprise."

"That was a smoke screen. I was just too chickenshit to give Jack advance warning in case he told me not to bother. So, yeah, go ahead and announce that I'll be in after I park the truck, but please tell Sarah I'm not planning to stay and interfere with this night of beauty she's set up."

Olivia looked amused. "I'll tell her. But don't blame me if she vetoes your decision." Then she shut the door, ending any further debate on the matter.

Pulling carefully away from the front of the house so he didn't accidentally take out a chunk of the wooden steps, he drove over to the area where everyone else had parked and turned off the engine. So he was here. Considering he'd met Olivia, he was glad he'd come.

But no matter what, he wouldn't stay at the ranch tonight. He'd made it out here, and he could make it back to the paved road, too. When Jack came home from the horse show tomorrow, Wyatt would drive over and try this routine again.

A flash of lightning followed by a crack of thunder that sounded like a mountain being split in two made him jump. The house went dark. Well, damn. What kind of guy marched into a house that had just lost power and announced he was taking off?

He needed to go in and find out what he could do to help before he left. Climbing out of the truck, he ignored the rain pelting him as he walked around to the rear and opened the back window of his camper shell. Fortunately his battery-operated lantern was within easy reach of the tailgate.

Lantern in hand, he sloshed through water and gravel and climbed the front steps. The cool, rain-scented air smelled of wood smoke, so a fire must be blazing inside. He unlaced his boots, toed them off and peeled away his wool socks, which were soaked.

When he came out—*if* he came out—he'd just wear the boots out to the truck and carry the socks. Taking a deep breath, he knocked on the door.

It opened soon afterward. "There you are!" Olivia stood holding a brass candlestick with a lit candle. She looked like an angel. "Come in. I told everyone who rescued me and they're all dying to meet you. Well, I guess Sarah has already met you."

"Briefly." He remembered a stately silver-haired woman in her sixties who had a warm smile and kind eyes. Stepping into the entryway, he closed the door behind him. "I'm dripping. I should stand out here on the mat for a minute so I don't mess up the hardwood floors." The musical hum of female voices and laughter filtered in from the living room, along with the clink of glasses and the snap and crackle of a fire.

"Maybe I should get you a towel."

"That's not necessary. I really can't stay." He threw the comment out there, although his escape hatch was closing fast. "But I brought a lantern in case the power's out for a while." He held it up.

"If the lightning hit a transformer, and Sarah thinks it might have, then the power will be out for the rest of the night."

"Doesn't the ranch have a backup generator for emergencies?"

"Yes, but it's not working right now. The men were planning to buy the part in Casper and repair it after they came back. I guess this storm was a surprise to everyone."

"Oh." Although intellectually Wyatt knew that the women on this ranch were unlikely to be helpless females who couldn't look after themselves during a power outage, he still couldn't picture himself driving away, knowing he'd left them in the middle of a blackout that might last until morning.

"Sarah wants you to stay, and I think you should. Pam's fine with it, and she won't charge you for a night at the Bunk and Grub, either."

The escape hatch closed with a bang. "I'm happy to pay her anyway, but yeah, I'll stay. Although I don't have anything with me like clothes and stuff. I left it all at the B and B."

"I'm sure that can be worked out. A place with this many men on-site must have some old clothes somewhere."

"I suppose." Wyatt felt something warm and wet on his bare feet. Glancing down, he discovered a low-slung, brown-and-white spotted dog with floppy ears licking his toes. "Who's this?"

"Rodney, Sarah's recently adopted dog. She got

him from a shelter in Colorado, and he's a mix but he's mostly basset hound."

"Not the kind of dog I'd expect on a ranch, but why not?" Wyatt crouched down and scratched behind the dog's oversized ears. "How's it going, Rodney?"

"His full name is Rodney Dangerfield."

Wyatt lifted the dog's muzzle and looked into his sad eyes. "Appropriate. Can't get no respect, can you, Rodney?"

The dog whined and wagged his white-tipped tail.

"You and me, we'll hang out tonight, buddy. We'll find us a baseball game on TV—"

"No power," Olivia said.

"Oh, right. No worries, Rod. With that face, I'll bet you're great at poker. We'll play cards by candlelight."

The dog whined again.

Olivia glanced up at him with a smile. "That's enough of the stall tactics. You've stopped dripping, so it's time to come inside and meet everyone. I told them how you rushed to my rescue, so I suspect you're going to be the man of the hour."

Wyatt groaned inwardly. Just what he didn't want. He followed Olivia into the living room with Rodney trotting at his heels. Wyatt wasn't sure of his welcome with Jack, but at least he'd scored with the dog.

3

OLIVIA GUESSED THAT WYATT had agreed to stay because he was unwilling to leave a group of ladies caught in a power outage. If chivalry kept him here, that was fine with her. She wouldn't mention that these were resourceful ranch women who didn't need a man to babysit them in an emergency.

But judging from what the women had said after she'd arrived, nobody should be out driving tonight, not even a can-do wilderness guide. Sarah's battery-operated weather radio had predicted high winds and hail would follow on the heels of the heavy rain. She and Wyatt walked into the living room, where a fire burned in the large rock fireplace and candles positioned around the room illuminated a comfortable collection of brown leather furniture and sturdy wooden side tables.

Conversation stopped among the eight women gathered there. Eleven-month-old Sarah Bianca, Morgan Chance's little girl who was known as "SB," continued to babble to her stuffed dinosaur, and four-month-old

Archie, Josie Chance's son, slept peacefully in his carrier. All other eyes turned toward Wyatt.

Olivia understood why. Firelight and candlelight bronzed his wet T-shirt look with an erotic glow that was truly mesmerizing. The women had good reason to stare, especially after hearing Olivia's tale of being carried through the rain by this fine specimen of manhood.

Sarah was the first to break the charged silence. "Good to see you again, Wyatt, but my goodness, you're soaked!" She set down her wineglass and walked toward him, all smiles. "We need to do something about that before you settle in."

Olivia swallowed a bubble of laughter. What Sarah really meant was that if she didn't reduce the sexual wattage of that impressive physique by giving him something dry to wear, the women would be distracted the entire evening by the resident beefcake.

"I have some of my sons' old clothes I was going to take to a rummage sale in town," Sarah said. "Come on back to the laundry room with me. Something should fit you."

"Thanks. I appreciate it." Wyatt set his lantern on a side table and followed her down the hallway to the left with Rodney close behind, his short legs moving rapidly to keep up.

"Whew." Josie Chance, Jack's wife, flipped her long, blond braid over her shoulder. "Don't anybody tell Jack I said so, but that guy's hot. I had no idea. Jack just said he was a typical hiker type with sandy-colored hair."

Morgan Chance, Josie's redheaded sister-in-law, laughed as she took the dinosaur her daughter handed her. "Of course he said that. You think he's going to describe his half brother, or any guy, for that matter, as good-looking?"

"I wish I could have snapped off a couple of shots before Sarah dragged him away." Nick Chance's wife, Dominique, a tall brunette with short hair, was a professional photographer who always had her camera handy. "But that would have spooked him, I'll bet."

"Oh, you think?" Mary Lou, who'd been a cook at the ranch for years, shook her head and grinned. "You ladies better take it down a notch or he's liable to spend the evening in a back room playing with the dog."

"That would be a shame." Olivia had returned to setting up her mani-pedi station in a corner, but she glanced over at Dominique. "Still, I would have loved a picture of him in that wet T-shirt. I can see it framed and hanging in your gallery. You'd sell a few prints of those, girlfriend."

"But you and Dominique would be the only ones who could get away with having that picture," said Tyler, Morgan's dark-haired sister. "I don't think Alex would take kindly to me pasting it up on the inside of my closet door. Those days are over for this married lady."

Emily, a petite blonde, lifted her chin. "I don't need a picture like that. I have Clay."

"Spoken like a woman who's only been a bride for two months." Morgan winked at her. "Just because we ogle once in a while doesn't mean we don't adore our guys. There's no harm in a little recreational voyeurism. Right, ladies?"

"Right!" everyone chorused, except for Emily.

"I can't believe I didn't recognize his name when he made his reservation at the Bunk and Grub." Pam Mulholland, a curvy woman who counted on Olivia to keep her gray hair looking blond, sipped her wine. "Sarah told me about his visit last summer, and you'd think I'd have made the connection."

"It's probably just as well you didn't." Josie walked over to peek at a still-sleeping Archie before retrieving her glass of mineral water. "If Jack had known he was coming, that might have changed his plans for the Casper horse show."

"True," Morgan said. "And I think it's great that they all went and took so many Last Chance horses. Gabe was looking forward to putting on a cutting horse demonstration."

"And Jack didn't have time to get all discombobulated at the idea of Wyatt returning," Josie added. "So I'm glad it didn't occur to you, Pam."

"I'm certainly not complaining, either." Olivia pulled her stainless-steel footbath out of one of her zippered totes. She'd organized the area with a comfy chair and a small desk for manicures and a second cozy chair for pedicures. She'd roll back and forth on the office chair Sarah had brought out.

"I'll bet you're not complaining," Morgan said.

"He seems really nice." As Olivia took inventory of the stack of towels Sarah had provided, she almost mentioned that Wyatt might move his business here, but she thought better of it. He wanted to relocate, but he might not appreciate having her give out that information prematurely.

"Yes, he does seem nice," Josie said. "I hope that everything—well, never mind. I hear them coming back down the hall."

"So!" Sarah clapped her hands together as she walked into the living room with Wyatt and the ever-present Rodney Dangerfield. "Let's get this party started!"

Olivia straightened and turned toward Sarah and Wyatt. Whoa. She was more than ready to party, all right, but she wished it could be a private one featuring her and the hunk of burning love who'd just walked in. The wet T-shirt had showcased Wyatt's glorious muscles beautifully, and she hadn't thought Sarah could improve on that.

Oh, but she had. The yoked gray Western shirt was a smidgen too tight and tucked into worn jeans that fit like a second skin...ooo, baby. Olivia licked her suddenly dry lips.

A scuffed but serviceable tooled leather belt with a plain silver buckle brought her attention to the fly of his jeans, and she looked away quickly before she could be caught staring. A pair of Western boots that showed some wear completed the outfit. He'd left the room a wilderness guide. He'd returned a cowboy.

SARAH INTRODUCED WYATT to everyone and he did his level best to keep them all straight. Josie, Jack's wife, would be important to remember. She was the one with the long blond braid. Their baby, Wyatt's new nephew, was named Archie, after Jack's grandfather. Archie was asleep in his carrier, so despite Wyatt's curiosity, he kept his distance, not wanting to wake him.

Morgan, a busty redhead, was obviously the mother of a little redheaded tot named Sarah Bianca, SB for short. Morgan's dark-haired sister, Tyler, had married

Alex Keller, Josie's brother. Wyatt decided when he had access to paper and pencil he'd write some of this down.

Then he met Dominique, a tall brunette who was the third daughter-in-law, and Emily, a petite blonde who had just married the guy who ran the stud program. That took care of the women in his generation.

He recognized Pam, a blonde in her fifties, from hearing her voice on the phone when he'd registered at the Bunk and Grub. By process of elimination he knew that the gray-haired woman with the jolly smile had to be Mary Lou, the cook. Yes, he would definitely write all this down before he went to sleep tonight.

But he should be okay for the evening while the introductions were fresh in his mind. Maybe this wouldn't be so awkward after all. He'd thought he'd be uncomfortable wearing somebody else's clothes but he'd been wrong. These cowboy duds felt great.

Sarah had offered him several shirts and pairs of jeans along with clean underwear. Neither of them had talked about the need for underwear, but he was soaked through.

Once Sarah had handed over the clothes, she'd waited outside the laundry room while he tried them on. He'd chosen the first things he'd put on for expediency's sake. But the longer he wore them, the more right they seemed.

When he'd asked her who the clothes had belonged to, she'd confided that they'd all been Jack's. Now that Jack was relaxed, happy and enjoying married life, he'd put on a little weight and couldn't wear them anymore without straining the seams. She'd made Wyatt promise not to mention the weight gain to Jack, because he swore the clothes had shrunk in the wash.

Apparently Wyatt was about the size that Jack had been a year ago, before he'd married Josie. Knowing they were so alike in build, if not in coloring, had pleased Wyatt. But meeting Jack while wearing his old clothes might be weird. Wyatt planned to drive back to the Bunk and Grub and change into his own stuff before Jack came home.

In the meantime, he liked the way Olivia had looked at him when he'd first come into the room. He hadn't thought about whether she had a soft spot in her heart for cowboys, and if so, he might decide to brush up on his riding skills and pick up some Western wear of his own. Re-creating that sparkle in her blue eyes would be worth the effort.

Sarah finished the introductions and turned to Olivia. "So who would you like to do first?"

In what looked like a purely unconscious move, Olivia glanced at Wyatt, and he swore he could read her X-rated response. Heat rocketed through him. Wow. He was definitely buying Western clothes before he left town.

She turned bright red before she looked away. "Why don't I start on Josie's nails while little Archie is asleep?"

"That's fine with me, but he sleeps through anything," Josie said. "But I guess if you do my nails first, they'll be dry in case he does wake up."

"I just thought of something." Sarah looked worried as she glanced at Olivia. "You'll want warm water for your finger bowl and the foot bath. The hot water heater's electric, so we have hot water now, but we won't for the rest of the evening."

"We can hang a kettle over the fire like people did in the old days," Mary Lou said.

Sarah brightened. "Sure we can. Problem solved. Let's get that kettle going now so it'll be ready when the water from the heater turns cool."

Talk of manicures and footbaths galvanized Wyatt into action. "I think it's about time for me to take Rodney and vamoose."

"Oh, no, you don't." Mary Lou smiled at him. "Now that we're in full swing, I could use some help getting the food laid out."

"We can help, Mary Lou," Dominique said. "Morgan has her hands full with SB, but the rest of us can schlep things from the kitchen."

"Hey, I'm glad to do it," Wyatt said. "I'm the party crasher around here, so it would make me feel better if I can be useful."

Dominique put down her wineglass. "Okay, but we can still help."

"Absolutely," Tyler said. "I'm actually good at this kind of thing."

"Ladies, ladies." Mary Lou held up both hands. "Your offer is much appreciated, but I think you should let this nice young man do the honors. I've had my eye on him since he walked in. I said to myself, *Oh, good. There's our muscle.*"

Wyatt pretended not to hear the muffled laughter that followed that remark. "Then it's settled. Everybody relax and I'll handle it." Considering how hungry he was and how many delicious smells had invaded the laundry room while he was changing clothes, he was more than willing to facilitate the food situation. He could always disappear after the meal part.

"Great," Mary Lou said. "Come on back and I'll show you where the large folding tables are stored. We need a couple set up in the living room so we can create a buffet. That way everyone can munch whenever they feel like it. Since the stove's electric, I need to move the hot food into chafing dishes and bring them out here."

"Sounds like a plan." Wyatt was aware of everyone eyeing him with amusement.

"Oh, and I'd appreciate it if you'd bring that light of yours into the kitchen, too."

"Sure thing." Wyatt grabbed the lantern from where he'd left it and followed Mary Lou down the same hall he'd recently traveled with Sarah. The left wall was a bank of windows, which now looked out on rain and streaks of lightning. But each time the lightning flashed, it lit up the other wall, which was covered with framed photos.

"What are all those pictures?" Wyatt asked.

"Family." Mary Lou kept walking. "No sense in trying to show you now, though. We'd have to use your lantern and we should probably conserve the batteries. But the entire history of the Chance family is there in those pictures."

"I'd like to study that." His mother would never allow a wall of pictures to spoil her ultrachic decor.

"I'm sure you would. Come down in the morning and I'll give you a guided tour." Mary Lou kept walking, but she glanced over at him. "I wish you well, Wyatt Locke. Your mother caused a lot of pain in this family but that's not your fault. It took guts for you to come back here, and that tells me you'd fit in a lot better than Diana ever did." She caught her breath. "Oh, I shouldn't have said that. It wasn't respectful. I'm sorry."

"Don't be sorry. I know my mother's not a popular person around the ranch." He hesitated, torn between truth and disloyalty. "She's a complicated woman. Being her son hasn't always been easy."

"Well said." Mary Lou reached over and patted his arm. "I personally think you'll be good for Jack. I only hope he'll be good for you, too."

"We'll see, Mary Lou. We'll see."

After that they didn't have time for philosophical discussions. Wyatt carried the folding banquet tables back down the hall and set them up while Mary Lou used his battery-operated lantern to light her work space in the kitchen. Because the ranch was used to serving hot food outdoors for barbecues, Mary Lou had an assortment of warming pans heated by gel packs instead of electricity.

As Wyatt helped her bring in the food, he laughed at his assumption that it would be finger sandwiches and tea cakes. This was hearty ranch fare—baked beans, ears of corn, coleslaw, fried chicken, mashed potatoes and a giant platter of chocolate frosted brownies for dessert. The only nod to what Wyatt considered girly food was a big bowl of salad and a relish tray of carrot sticks, celery, radishes, pickles and green onions.

Sarah told Wyatt where to find a high chair for little SB, and he brought that in along with an oil cloth he spread under it to catch food fallout. Then he helped Morgan settle the little redheaded girl into her seat, along with her stuffed dinosaur and a bowlful of dry Cheerios. He'd never spent much time around little kids and he was surprised that he instinctively took to it.

Mary Lou announced the food was ready and the women didn't hold back. Laughing and talking, they loaded their plates and refilled their wineglasses. Wyatt, being gentlemanly and an uninvited guest, waited until they'd all gone through the line. That included Olivia, who'd finished Josie's manicure.

"I'll fix your plate for you," Olivia said to Josie. "You need to be careful of your fingernails."

"I can do it for Josie," Wyatt said. "You go ahead and eat, Olivia."

"Why, thank you." She gave him such a dazzling smile that he temporarily forgot what he'd volunteered for. He was fascinated by that tiny space between her front teeth. Adorable.

"You're making points fast," Josie said to him. "Gallantry counts around here. Are you sure you're not a cowboy?"

When she spoke, he refocused on his task and picked up a plate. "My brother and I used to pretend to be cowboys when we were kids." He grabbed a napkin and utensils, too. "Does that count?"

"Absolutely." She pointed to the steaming baked beans. "Lots of those, please. Light on the potatoes and heavy on the coleslaw."

Wyatt loaded Josie's plate as instructed and carried it over to an empty chair next to the baby carrier sitting on the floor. Archie slept on, despite the racket.

After making sure Josie was all set and hadn't ruined

her manicure, Wyatt crouched down next to the baby carrier. "Looks like he took after you more than Jack."

"I think so." Josie gazed with fondness at her son. "He has Jack's nose, though, and of course he's only four months. His blond hair could get darker, but he definitely didn't inherit Jack's coloring."

Wyatt studied the tiny face, so sweet and soft. Something about the nose reminded him of Rafe's baby pictures. "He looks…familiar."

"He should. You're related to him." Josie laid down her fork and looked at Wyatt. "I hope you'll be patient with my husband. He puts his shields up when it comes to you, even though it's not your fault that your mother…well…"

"Abandoned him." Wyatt met her gaze. "It's okay. You can say it. There's no good excuse for what she did and I promise I won't try to make any."

"I'm sure that will help. At one time I thought Jack had accepted his past, but meeting you has stirred it up again. Unfortunately I think he resents the fact that she started another family while continuing to pretend he didn't exist."

Guilt pricked him. "I don't want to create problems."

"You're not the one who created the problem. Diana did. Jack knows about you and your brother now, so you can't put the toothpaste in the tube again. Coming back was the right move, in my opinion."

"Thanks, Josie. Jack's a lucky guy to have you."

"We're lucky to have each other," she said softly. Then her glance shifted as she looked over his shoulder. "Too bad you can't see the expression on Olivia's face right now. Women get all mushy when they see a guy crouched down next to a baby."

Warmth crept up the back of his neck and he resisted the urge to turn around. "But I wasn't doing it for—"

"I know. I can see that you're the real deal, Wyatt. Olivia can, too. We all can. Even Rodney."

Upon hearing his name, the dog padded over and pushed his nose against Wyatt's leg. Wyatt ran a hand over the dog's silky head. "Yeah, I know, Rod. I promised you we'd hang out and here I am ignoring you."

Josie chuckled. "Now Olivia's *really* got a sappy look on her face. Kids and dogs. I'm telling you, Wyatt, you have a gift. Not that it's any of my business, but is there a girl back home?"

"No, actually, there's not. I've been pretty busy getting my business up and running."

"In that case, I suggest you grab a plate of food and go sit by Olivia while she has a moment to herself."

Wyatt smiled. "Believe I will. Come on, Rod. Apparently you're an asset to the cause."

As Wyatt headed to the buffet table, Mary Lou handed him a cold bottle of beer. "Most times the guys prefer this to wine," she said.

"Thanks, Mary Lou."

"There's more where that came from. I brought in a small cooler and put it under the table. Consider it your reward for all your fine work."

"You're a gem." He tucked the beer in the crook of his arm, filled a plate with food, and walked over to where Olivia sat on a leather-covered ottoman.

She glanced up, welcome in her blue eyes. "Hi, there. I'd offer you a seat, but there isn't one."

"No worries." Setting his plate on a nearby end table, he crouched down next to her. Rodney took a spot right by his feet. "I'm used to making do." He unscrewed the cap on his beer and took a swallow. "That's quite a spread Mary Lou put on."

"See, I told you to stay for the food."

He didn't say what he was thinking, that he'd eat twigs and leaves if he could be near her while doing it. "You were right." He noticed that Rodney was staring up at him as if he hadn't had a decent meal in a week. "The dog thinks so, too."

"Don't feed him anything. Sarah has him on a special diet. He's overweight."

"How can you tell with a basset hound? They're all sort of roly-poly."

"Beats me, but she wants him to be able to fit into his life vest and it's still a little tight."

Wyatt blinked. "His *what?*"

"One reason she wanted to adopt him, besides the fact he's adorable, was his tracking ability. Sarah's always wanted a tracking dog on the ranch. Butch and Sundance, the two mixed breeds living down in the barn, aren't particularly good trackers."

"So what's that got to do with a life vest?"

"There are streams and ponds all over the property, and basset hounds can't swim. Their bones are too dense."

"They are?" Wyatt looked down at Rodney. "I didn't know that."

"Me either, but Sarah researched it. If she wants to turn him loose to do his tracking, he has to wear a life vest so he won't accidentally fall in the water and drown."

Wyatt took another swig of his beer and glanced down at Rodney. "I'm getting quite a visual here, Rod. I'm thinking YouTube video star, aren't you?"

Olivia laughed. "I think you're on to something. Definitely bring a camcorder next time you come to the ranch." She picked up her empty plate and stood. "Well, time for me to get back to work. You can have the ottoman."

Wyatt rose, too. "Actually, I think I'll take my plate, my beer and the dog into the kitchen. I'll just be in the way out here."

"I heard that." Morgan, little SB on her hip, walked toward him. "Don't think you can sneak out of here that easy. I'm sure I speak for everyone when I say we'd love for you to hang around."

"Yes, we definitely would," said Dominique from her spot on one of the couches.

Wyatt wasn't sure where this was headed. He glanced over at Olivia, but she was already settled into her chair and preparing for her next customer. "Hey, I'll just cramp your style," he said to the room in general. "Rodney and I will be fine in the kitchen, right, Rod?"

The dog gave him a doleful look.

"Our style isn't that easily cramped," Morgan said. "And we need somebody to tend the fire and add wood. We'll all have fresh manicures and can't do that." She looked up at him. "Unless you're planning to get a manicure, too, in which case we—"

"I'm not getting a manicure."

"See? So you'd be perfect, then. Instead of a designated driver we need a designated fire tender."

Wyatt had to hand it to these Chance women. They were very good at maneuvering a guy into doing what they wanted. "Then I'd be honored to watch the fire for you."

"Excellent." Morgan beamed at him. "Besides, it's not every day we get the opportunity to talk to a single guy without our husbands around to kibitz."

He gave her a wary look. "Talk about what?"

"What else?" Morgan's green eyes twinkled. "Men!"

4

Olivia almost felt sorry for Wyatt, who looked somewhat like a cornered animal. But he was a big boy, and besides, she was curious to see how this would turn out.

"I'm not sure what you mean," he said.

"Let me explain." Morgan shifted SB to her other hip. "Most of us in this room are married, and the ones who aren't are getting closer by the day."

"Not true," Mary Lou said. "I'm never marrying that old fool Watkins, and you can quote me on that."

"Emmett still has a burr under his saddle about the size of my bank account," Pam said. "So I don't see us tying the knot anytime soon, either."

All attention focused on Sarah, the remaining single lady other than Olivia. Sarah was blushing.

Morgan paused expectantly. "Well? Do you have news at long last?"

She cleared her throat. "I guess it's okay to say something."

Dominique laughed. "At this point, I think it's required to say something, Sarah. We're all dying of curiosity. Have been for months."

"Well, Pete and I have talked about it, but we haven't set an actual—"

Squeals of joy erupted as everyone ran over to hug Sarah. Olivia, who didn't feel she knew Sarah quite well enough to be part of the hug fest, motioned Wyatt over to the manicure table so she could fill him in on the meaning of the uproar.

He walked over, carrying his beer. "Who's Pete?"

"Peter Beckett. He's a local philanthropist. He and Sarah put together a youth program that begins here in two weeks. They'll be boarding several problem teens and giving them a chance to work at the ranch for the summer."

Wyatt's eyes widened. "Hey, that's cool."

"It is. Really cool. And everyone's suspected a romance between the two of them, but Sarah always denied it before."

"She looks happy. Is this Peter guy good enough for her?"

"Her sons all like him, so I'd say he has the Chance stamp of approval."

Emotion flickered in Wyatt's soft gray eyes. "I have a feeling that's not so easy to get."

"Don't worry. It'll work out between you and Jack." She gazed up at him. "You already have a lot of support right in this room."

"I hope so. I'd enjoy being part of life around here."

"Even when you're about to be put on the hot seat?"

"Yeah." He massaged the back of his neck. "I'm not sure what that's all about."

"After all my years as a beautician listening to women talk, I can make an educated guess. Husbands are more prone to say what they think their wives want to hear. These gals are hoping you might actually tell them the truth about what guys are thinking."

"But it's only one point of view."

"Yes, but you've established yourself as one of the good guys and that makes your point of view worth exploring." She pushed back her chair. "I'll get you another beer. That should help."

Before he could protest, she'd hurried over to the buffet table and snagged another bottle out of the ice-filled cooler Mary Lou had brought in.

"Here." She handed it to him and then stepped closer. "Listen, before I make a complete fool of myself, I need to ask you something."

"What's that?"

"Are you involved with anyone?"

He looked into her eyes and his gaze was straightforward. "Nope, I'm not. Not at all. Are you?"

"Not yet." Rising up on tiptoe, she gave him another one of her drive-by kisses. She was fast becoming obsessed with his mouth, but she didn't dare linger. "I have to refresh my soaking solution." She picked up the crystal bowl she used for that purpose and headed toward a bathroom located just down the hall on the right.

If she'd ever met a more adorable guy than Wyatt, she couldn't recall who it might have been. If he truly wanted to relocate to Shoshone, Wyoming, she'd do whatever she could to help him make that happen.

ONCE AGAIN, OLIVIA HAD GOTTEN the drop on him. Wyatt vowed that the next time he'd be ready for her when she did that and he'd get in some lip pressure of his own.

In the meantime, he stood there holding one full bottle of beer and one nearly empty one while he gazed after her like some love-struck adolescent. He finished off the almost-empty beer and looked for a place to put the bottle.

"I'll take that." Morgan appeared at his elbow with her red-haired mini-me propped on her hip. "You need to finish your meal because we really do have some burning questions."

If Wyatt had hoped Morgan had forgotten her original plan in the flurry of excitement over Sarah's admission, that hope was now officially dashed. "I'm really not very knowledgeable about—"

"Now don't be modest, Wyatt. You're eligible and you're gorgeous, which puts you in the perfect position to give us some insight into how guys think these days." She gestured to an empty chair. "That seat's available. I'll be right back."

Wyatt glanced over at Olivia, who'd just started working on Pam Mulholland's nails. Olivia looked up with an encouraging smile. She'd told him he had support in this room, so maybe he should stick around. Retrieving his plate, he sat in the chair Morgan had indicated and began to eat. He probably needed to keep up his strength.

With a little doggy sigh, Rodney plopped down on the floor beside him.

Kids and dogs. Wyatt realized he hadn't had much to do with either because his mother hadn't wanted any messes in her perfectly decorated house. All his playing as a kid had been at the school yard or somebody else's place.

Pets hadn't been an option either. Once Wyatt became a wilderness guide, he'd given up any thoughts of getting a dog even though he no longer lived with his mother. He traveled too much. But if he was based in Shoshone and was welcome at the ranch, he could interact with the dogs and horses here.

As he was polishing off the last of his dinner, Morgan sat in the chair next to his and settled her daughter, who was drifting off to sleep against her shoulder. "Okay. I get the first question. Inquiring minds want to know…what's the most important thing a man looks for in a woman?"

"For what?" He figured hedging was a good tactic.

"For anything. Conversation, working together, bedroom games, whatever."

"I can only speak for myself."

Tyler, Morgan's dark-haired sister, dropped onto a sofa nearby. "Tonight, my friend, you're speaking for every man."

Wyatt took a fortifying sip of his beer, which bought him a little more time to think. Finally he settled on his answer. "Enthusiasm."

"Can you be more specific?" Tyler combed her dark hair back from her face. "Enthusiasm for what, exactly?"

"I think he's talking about sex," Morgan said. "You are, aren't you, Wyatt?"

"Not just sex." He slugged back some more beer. "It's fun to be with someone who goes all in with whatever she's doing. And sure, that goes for sex, too, but—"

"I think he means sex," Pam called over from the manicure station.

"Not *only* sex." Wyatt sat forward in his chair and gestured with his beer bottle. "I'm talking about enthusiasm for her work, and if she plays any sports then I hope she plays them with all she's got. If she has hobbies then I hope she loves doing them. I want her to be passionate about whatever she's doing."

"I'm here to tell you I'm not enthusiastic about housework," Dominique said.

"That's something I think men should be enthusiastic about." Josie held her hands out in front of her and gazed admiringly at her pink fingernails. "Then maybe this manicure would last awhile."

"Wyatt." Morgan gazed at him. "Do you clean your own place?"

"Uh, yeah." He felt a trap was about to be sprung.

"Enthusiastically?" Tyler asked.

"Not exactly, but—"

"Aha!" Dominique pointed a finger at him.

Wyatt glanced over at the fire. "Gee, will you look at that? I need to tend the fire. If you'll all excuse me." Setting his empty beer bottle down, he stood and walked over to the fireplace.

"Be sure and tend it enthusiastically!" Morgan called after him, which made everyone laugh.

"Oh, you know it, ladies." As he moved the screen aside, he started whistling some snappy tune he'd heard recently on the radio. He often whistled on long drives to amuse himself, so he was pretty good at it by now. Then he added a few dance steps when he picked up a log from the rack beside the fireplace. The women began clapping rhythmically.

At that point he felt he had no choice. Instead of

backing off, which any sane or less inebriated man would have done, he turned the fire building into a hip-swinging, foot-stomping routine worthy of Chippendales. He'd never actually seen a Chippendales routine but this was how he thought it might go, minus the logs and the fireplace tools.

Where he got the inspiration was a mystery, although it might have been the beer he'd had. It also might have something to do with Olivia being in the room. He wanted her to know he was up to the challenge thrown down by these women.

He finished with a flourish that won him loud applause. Amazingly, both babies slept through the whole thing. He met Olivia's gaze for one quick moment and had to look away. She'd obviously liked the performance, and that sizzle passing between them was liable to attract unwanted attention.

Returning to his chair, he sank into it gratefully.

"Well done," Morgan said.

"Relax and have another beer." Dominique brought it to him this time. "Girls, let's stop picking on the poor guy for a while. He's acquitted himself admirably, and besides, we have brownies to eat."

"And beauty to accomplish." Josie smiled at Wyatt. "You should at least have Olivia give you a pedicure."

"I don't think so." When Olivia finally touched him, he didn't want her to start with his feet.

"Maybe he'd agree to just a foot massage," Olivia called over from the manicure table. "I give great foot massages."

He'd just bet she did. The thought spiked his blood pressure because anyone who gave good foot massages was into sensuous contact of all kinds. He shifted his weight in the chair and told himself not to think about it.

"Pam's done," Olivia said. "Who wants to be next?"

Mary Lou waved her hand in the air. "I'd love a pedicure."

"Then come on down, Mary Lou." Olivia stood and squirted some liquid soap into the stainless-steel bowl in front of the second chair. "I'll go fill the footbath."

"No, *I'll* fill the footbath." Wyatt left his seat and walked over to take the bowl from her. He hadn't given enough thought to how much work this night would be for Olivia. He couldn't paint nails, but he could fetch water.

"Thanks." The look in her eyes told him he'd done a good thing.

"Any instructions?"

"Test the temperature on your wrist. It should feel warm but not scalding. I think the water coming from the faucet in the tub should still be warm enough, but if it's not, leave room so I can add some from the fireplace kettle."

"Got it." Following her directions, he soon returned with a sudsy pan of water, which he placed carefully in front of the chair where Mary Lou already sat barefoot with an eager expression on her lined face. She immersed both feet with a sigh of pleasure. "Thank you, Wyatt."

"I'll be in charge of the footbath from now on, Olivia."

From the group of women gathered in the seating area came a long, drawn-out "Awww."

"I swear to God, Wyatt," Tyler said. "You are redefining the word *hero*."

"I have to admit he's setting the bar pretty high," Josie said. "I—" She paused as the theme song from *Pirates of the Caribbean* started playing. "That would be Jack on my cell."

Wyatt tensed as Josie located her purse, pulled the phone out and answered it. Holding the phone to her ear, she talked quietly as she stood and walked down the hall he'd just come from. In an instant he went from feeling welcome and appreciated to thinking of himself as an intruder.

Conversation flowed again after the interruption, and Wyatt joined in as if that phone call didn't occupy ninety-nine percent of his thoughts. Josie would mention his arrival. It was the right thing to do in an open and forthright relationship, and Wyatt believed Josie and Jack had that.

Fortunately for Wyatt's sanity the call was short. Josie walked back into the room looking calm. That was promising, he told himself.

"Is everything going well in Casper?" Morgan asked.

"Very well. They've sold several horses and Clay's written up quite a few orders for semen delivery."

Emily's face seemed lit from within. "That's so great. He had high hopes for this trip and I'm so happy for him. Well, and for the Last Chance, of course."

"That is good news," Sarah said. "How's the weather down there?"

"Not bad at all, and that's why Jack called. He heard about the storm hitting Jackson Hole and wanted to know how we were doing. I told him the power was out but we were coping fine." She looked at Wyatt. "And of course I told him you were here."

Wyatt's gut tensed. "What did he say to that?"

"Not much." Her voice gentled. "But that's Jack. He's not chatty on the phone. He said he'd be home late tomorrow afternoon."

Wyatt nodded. "It'll be good to see him." At least Jack hadn't said that Wyatt had better be gone by then.

5

By the time Olivia had finished six manicures and three pedicures she should have been exhausted, but having Wyatt around kept her energy level high. For one thing, he insisted on emptying and refilling the footbath and the soak bowl, which saved her some time and effort. But just looking across the room and exchanging a glance with him was enough to recharge her batteries whenever she started to drag.

Besides helping her, he carried the chafing dishes back to the kitchen once everyone had finished eating, took down the folding tables and worked with Mary Lou on cleanup duty. After Archie woke up and was fed and changed, Wyatt took a turn at holding the little guy.

Although holding a baby seemed to make him nervous to begin with, soon he relaxed and began making faces at Archie. That activity entertained both the baby and the women gathered around sipping the last of their wine and exclaiming over the beauty of their nails.

Olivia finished her last manicure, a pale peach shade for Emily, and began packing up her supplies. Rain still pounded on the roof and slashed at the windows. Sarah had called down to the bunkhouse and the few hands who were there reported that the horses were fine and the barn didn't seem to be leaking, so they were all going to bed.

Olivia had brought pajamas and a change of clothes, but she didn't know where Sarah planned for her to sleep. One of the recently constructed bunks upstairs would be fine. Growing up in the chaotic household of an eccentric father had made her flexible when it came to sleeping accommodations.

As if reading Olivia's mind, Sarah set down her empty wineglass and stood. "I see some droopy eyelids, and I'm about ready to turn in myself."

Josie yawned. "Yep. It's been great, but I'm ready for some shut-eye."

"Go on up whenever you want." Sarah waved a hand at the upper floor. "The only ones who don't know where they're bunking down are Wyatt and Olivia, so now would be an excellent time for me to show them." She picked up a candle sheltered inside a small glass chimney. "Come on upstairs, you two."

Olivia knew Sarah hadn't meant to link them together as if they'd be sleeping in the same room, but the image stuck in her mind anyway. She didn't know Wyatt well enough to sleep with him…yet. But she intended to further the acquaintance. All the signs pointed to the possibility that something wonderful could develop between them.

Leaving her tidying, she stood and followed Sarah toward the wide, winding staircase. Archie Chance, little Archie's great-grandfather, had been a master carpenter who'd constructed the graceful wooden stairway leading to the second floor. Olivia had wanted to climb that staircase from the first time she'd seen it, which had been at Emily and Clay's wedding.

That day she'd had no reason to go upstairs. But now she had a chance to sleep in one of the rooms and she was thrilled about it, even if she wouldn't be sharing with Wyatt. The Last Chance Ranch house seemed like the height of casual elegance to her.

Wyatt was right behind her on the stairs, and she was superaware of that fact. The attraction between them seemed to be growing rapidly, at least from her perspective, and sleeping under the same roof tonight would be tantalizing. She wouldn't allow anything to happen and she doubted he would either, but the forced proximity heated her blood.

Sarah reached the landing and waited for them both to join her. "As Olivia knows, we've converted some of these rooms to dormitory-style spaces to accommodate the teenagers who are coming—God help us all—in two weeks."

"Olivia told me about that." Wyatt stood close, but not so close as to imply they were a couple. "I love that idea."

Olivia imagined she could feel his body heat, but that was probably her hyperawareness kicking in. "I'd be perfectly happy in a bunk," she said. "Put me wherever."

"Actually, the others are in the dorm spaces. They all know each other so well, so I assigned Morgan and Josie to one room, along with a couple of portable cribs for SB and Archie. Dominique, Tyler and Emily are in another dorm room. Pam's downstairs with me and Mary Lou has her own apartment off the kitchen."

Olivia would have been happy to squeeze in with the other women, but this was Sarah's call, so she kept quiet.

"So I'm putting you in Roni's old room, Olivia. That's one we decided not to convert, so you have your own bath attached."

"Roni's the mechanic for a NASCAR team, right?" Olivia was grateful for all the gossip in the salon, which had filled her in on the players at the Last Chance.

"That's her, the runaway teen we took in years ago. Come to think of it, she kind of foreshadowed this program Pete and I have created." Surrounded by the glow of her candle, Sarah started down the hall to her right. "Occasionally Roni comes home for a visit and brings her husband, Judd, with her, so we like to keep her room available. But it's yours for the night." She reached a doorway on the right side of the hall, stepped inside and lifted the candle up. "I think it'll work for you."

Olivia glanced into the room and could make out a race car motif on the bedspread covering the double bed and repeated in the curtains and the pictures hanging on the walls. It wasn't her style but she didn't care. Any room at the Last Chance was special.

"It's perfect," she said. "Thank you for putting me up."

Sarah stepped back into the hall and wrapped an arm around her shoulders. "Thank you for agreeing to participate in our little party. Everyone had fun, and our nails look fabulous."

"I was happy to do it, Sarah." But now Olivia couldn't help but wonder where Wyatt would be sleeping. Considering that she'd be in this wing with the other women, she had a suspicion…

"I'm putting you in the other wing, Wyatt," Sarah said.

Bingo. That would have been Olivia's guess. Underneath it all, Sarah had a touch of old-fashioned propriety, and Olivia respected that. She wasn't about to violate the unspoken rules.

"Anywhere is fine," Wyatt said.

"You're going to be in Jack's old room." Sarah walked to the other side of the house, with Olivia and Wyatt trailing behind. "Eventually we may turn this side of the house into dorm rooms, too, but for now they're just guest rooms. Jack's enormous bed is gone but I bought something to replace it." She held the candle aloft once again.

Olivia released a little sigh of pleasure. In the pool of candlelight she could see that the room was furnished in soft greens and browns—a man's room, and yet the kind of room a woman would love to slip into and be seduced by that man. Olivia repressed a tug of longing and promised herself that she would not, would *not,* lie in bed tonight and picture Wyatt stretched out under that fluffy hunter-green quilt wearing…probably nothing. He had no clothes of his own here, and anyway, he didn't seem like the pajama type.

"It's a very nice room," Wyatt said. "I'll only be here one night, of course, but thanks for letting me—"

"Don't be silly." Sarah turned to him. "You're family, and I won't have you paying for a room somewhere else, even if it's in Pam's B and B. I've already discussed it with her and she's fine with having you move over here."

"But I just appeared, without notice," Wyatt protested. "You shouldn't feel the least bit obligated to put me up under the circumstances."

"It's not a matter of obligation," Sarah said gently. "It's a matter of welcoming those who are related to us." She paused. "And much as I hesitate to say this, that would go for your mother if she were inclined to visit."

Olivia's breath caught. Really? Sarah would house Diana under her roof?

"I would never expect that of you," Wyatt said. "That you would even say such a thing speaks to your generosity of spirit, but my mother has forfeited any right to stay in this house."

"You're wrong." Sarah's voice was low but firm and her gaze steady. "No matter what she's done, she's still Jack's mother and little Archie's grandmother. If it would help Jack heal the wounds that I'm afraid still fester in him, I would welcome the devil herself into my home."

Wyatt stared at her in silence for several seconds. "That might be an accurate description of Diana."

"Careful. She's your mother."

"I know. Believe me, I know."

The silence stretched between them.

"And Archie's grandmother." Sarah took a deep breath and shook her head. "I don't know what to do about that. After all, little Archie is her grandchild, more hers than mine if we're talking about a biological link."

"Blood isn't everything."

"No, but it counts."

"In this case I don't think it counts for much," Wyatt said. "I'd recommend keeping the baby info quiet for now. It's probably enough that Jack has to deal with me."

Sarah gave him a knowing smile. "Wise words." She glanced over at Olivia. "Bet you didn't expect to get mixed up in a family drama, did you?"

Olivia spoke from her heart. "I feel privileged that you've included me in the discussions, and I promise you I won't gossip about anything I've heard here."

"I know you won't. I trust you. But I'd hate to think we've made you the least bit uncomfortable by airing our dirty laundry."

"Not at all. Ever since I moved here, I've wanted to learn more about the Chance family. You're legendary in Shoshone."

Sarah's cheeks turned pink. "Well, I don't know about that."

"It's true, Sarah. Being asked to come out for Emily and Clay's wedding preparations was an honor considering I'd only been here for six months. When you suggested tonight's manicure party, I was thrilled. I can't imagine ever regretting the opportunity to be part of whatever's going on here."

Sarah's eyes had regained their old sparkle. "That's quite a compliment."

"I know what she means," Wyatt said. "I felt something special the minute I stepped inside the ranch house last summer. You've built something here that you should be proud of. Archie and SB represent the fourth generation of Chances on this land, right?"

"Yes, they do." Sarah couldn't hold back a smile of

satisfaction. "And I am proud of that. Archie and Nelsie would have loved knowing that we're still here." Her expression softened. "So would Jonathan. He'd be so proud of what his boys have accomplished since he's been gone."

"I wish I could have met him," Wyatt said.

"I wish you could have, too." Sarah appeared to consider that possibility for a moment, and then she shook her head and laughed. "No telling how he would have reacted to meeting you, though, so maybe we shouldn't think about that too wistfully. Anyway, we've delved into this mess enough for one night. Let's go back. I just wanted each of you to know where you were laying your weary heads tonight."

On the way downstairs they met Josie and Morgan coming up, each carrying her child. Morgan had located a flashlight and was using it to light their way. Wyatt stepped aside to give them more room to pass while Sarah and Olivia continued on down.

"We're packing it in," Morgan said. "The others are cleaning up the last few things before they come up. Pam's already gone off to her room, and I think Mary Lou's in bed by now. We tried to get Rodney to go out to pee, but he won't. We weren't sure if you were ready to bank the fire, either, so we left it."

"I can take care of the fire," Wyatt said. "I'll make sure it's okay before I go to bed. And I can take the dog out, too. Maybe it'll let up a little and he'll be more willing."

Sarah reached the bottom of the stairs and turned back to smile up at him. "That would be wonderful, on both counts. Thanks for all your help."

"Seems like the least I can do."

"You're a pleasure to have around, Wyatt." Sarah laid a hand on his arm once he joined her. "In fact, if your brother Rafe is anything like you, then—"

"He's not. He's a lot harder and tougher than I am, at least on the outside. When we were kids he was always telling me not to care so much."

Sarah nodded. "Sounds like Jack."

"If you put the two of them in a room together, you'd know they were brothers immediately. It's not only that they look so much alike, but they seem to have the same attitude."

"Which explains why you came to the ranch and he refused." Sarah gave his arm a pat. "I'm so glad you did."

"Me too."

"And now I'm off to bed. Sleep well, both of you." With a little wave, she headed down the hallway toward her room.

Dominique walked toward the stairs, trailed by a sleepy-looking Tyler and Emily holding candles. "We're going up, too," Dominique said. "Thanks for a fabulous job, Olivia."

"Yeah, thanks!" Tyler said. "Loved it."

"You're welcome, all of you."

"And thanks for the floor show, Wyatt," Emily added with a laugh.

"Anytime."

"The dog has to pee," Tyler said over her shoulder as she trudged upstairs. "We couldn't make him go out."

"We'll handle it," Olivia said.

"There's rain boots, slickers and a flashlight by the

front door!" Tyler called out before disappearing down the hall.

After the women were out of sight, Olivia took a deep breath before looking up at Wyatt. "I don't know about you, but I wouldn't mind relaxing by the fire a little longer."

"Listen, don't worry about me. I really can take care of the dog."

That wasn't quite the response she'd hoped for. Maybe he wasn't in the mood for company. "Or, maybe you'd prefer to sit by the fire alone."

"I didn't say that."

"Well, except for Rodney. Maybe you'd like to do the man and his dog companionship thing."

Alert to the sound of his name, the dog padded over and stood looking up at them.

"Olivia, I—"

"Or, maybe you'd like to toddle off to bed and let me take care of the fire and the dog. I used to have a dog, so I can handle Rodney. And my father's a scientist. I understand the principle of banking a fire."

That produced a smile. "Let's not bank the fire yet. Let's put on another log."

"Okay." Now, that was more like it.

"You haven't had a chance to put your feet up all night. I think I should give *you* a foot massage."

Her first thought was that would be heaven. Her second was that she was the foot care professional and Emily had suggested it would make a good payback for having him rescue her. "No, really, I should give you one in exchange for pulling me out of the ditch."

He rolled his eyes. "Tell you what. I'll massage your feet first, and then you can massage mine. How's that?"

"I like it."

"Good." He took her by the hand and led her to the couch with Rodney following behind. "Take off your shoes and get comfortable while I build up the fire."

"Gladly." She sank down to the soft leather cushions as he walked over to the hearth and moved the screen aside. "I enjoyed your floor show, too, by the way." She eased her shoes off.

"If that's a hint, I'm not putting on another one." He grabbed a log and laid it in the middle of the bed of embers. "Basically I'm too shy to do that, but I'd had a fair amount of beer on an empty stomach."

Damn, but he was cute. She had a serious crush going on, made more intense by that wounded part of him he tried so hard to hide. "I wasn't asking for a song and dance routine," she said. "I'd just like to talk and get to know you better."

He replaced the screen, dusted off his hands and turned back to her. "I'm all yours."

She knew he wasn't, not really. But he'd just stated her ultimate goal. She'd been too passive in her dating life and had allowed men to choose her. Then she'd gone along with their decision to become a couple. But for the first time in her life, she was making the choice, and she wanted Wyatt Locke.

6

WYATT COULDN'T IMAGINE a more beautiful sight than Olivia relaxing on the cushy leather couch, firelight dancing over her skin and gilding her curves as she waited for him to join her. He wished he'd met her under different circumstances, when he wasn't dealing with the emotional issue of his half brother, Jack. But if not for that issue, he might never have met Olivia at all.

He sat at the opposite end of the couch and turned to lean back against the rolled arm. Drawing his leg up onto the cushion, he reached for her left foot and brought it into his lap. Her sparkly toes rested inches from his crotch, but he vowed not to think about that.

"You'll have to give me some pointers." He took hold of her foot with both hands and ran his thumbs up the curve of her arch. "You're the professional."

"That feels nice. It's nearly impossible to do it wrong unless you're tentative. Firmness is everything."

He grinned. "Sort of like sex." Whoops. He hadn't really meant to introduce that topic. The words had slipped out, probably because he was thinking so hard about how they would not get sexual tonight. "Sorry. Shouldn't have brought that up."

"Why not?"

"Inappropriate." Cupping her heel in one hand, he began working on each individual toe. Touching her feet was great, but he couldn't help thinking how nice it would be to touch the rest of her.

"I wouldn't say that. Neither one of us is committed to anyone, and speaking for myself, I'm very attracted to you."

"I'm very attracted to you, too." He used a more gentle pressure as he rubbed the top of her foot. "But under the circumstances, we can't do anything about that. Not tonight, anyway."

Her expression grew serious. "No, we can't. I think Sarah made that clear when she put me on the girls' side of the house and you on the boys' side."

"Yeah, I got that message." He worked his fingers into the crevice at the base of her toes.

She moaned softly. "That feels terrific."

He chuckled. "Anybody listening might misinterpret that moan and comment, you know."

"Do you think anyone is?"

"Don't know. They all looked pretty tired to me."

She gave him a secret smile. "I think everyone's fast asleep, but just in case, I'll keep my moans discreet. You are doing a fabulous job, by the way. I suspect you've massaged a woman's feet before."

"A time or two." He concentrated on a spot next to the ball of her foot. When he'd first pushed against it, she'd looked almost orgasmic. And he didn't need to think about *that* subject, either.

He searched for a more general topic. "So, how many broken hearts did you leave back in Pittsburgh?"

"Three."

"Oh?" He hadn't expected such an instant and precise answer.

"At least I assume their hearts were broken—temporarily—and I'm truly sorry for that. My heart was broken, too, because I'm the perennial relationship optimist, so I convinced myself we were meant for each other. But just so you know, I always gave back the ring."

"The *ring?*" He was so startled he stopped rubbing her foot. "Are you saying you were engaged to all three of these guys?"

"I was. And each time I thought it was for keeps, but then…I realized it wasn't going to work, and I'd have to break off the engagement. Which was all terrible and sad for both of us."

"I'm sure it was." Knowing she'd accepted a marriage proposal three different times was sobering. Then she'd rejected each of those guys and returned the ring. He hoped never to have to go through something that painful.

She glanced down at her foot. "Ready to switch?"

Her revelation had made him completely forget about massaging her feet. "Um, yeah. I'll work on the other one now."

"I really appreciate this. I can't remember the last time a guy offered." She pulled her left foot back and gave him her right.

"I'm happy to do it." He wondered if any of her three ex-fiancés could have saved the day with a decent foot rub. He reapplied himself to the task at hand, but in the back of his mind he was still assimilating the fact that Olivia could commit and uncommit far more easily than he could. That was important to know.

"I think I figured out the problem, though, and I don't expect to go through that again."

"And what's the problem?" He pushed with both thumbs as he worked his way up her arch.

"Oh, that's *heaven.*" She closed her eyes. "Please do that again, Wyatt."

He did, but he was in serious trouble. She was turning him on with her breathless comments. He could see why her exes had become involved with her. He knew exactly why they'd shown up with a ring in their pocket and no doubt a *firmness,* as she'd put it, in their Jockeys.

She was beautiful and sensuous, which was attractive to most any man. Besides that, she had the quality he'd mentioned earlier while being grilled by the women. She was enthusiastic. And yes, he was thinking about sexual enthusiasm, damn it.

So what had she been talking about before she closed her eyes and moaned like a woman in the midst of sexual ecstasy? He searched his lust-soaked brain. Oh, yes.

And he really wanted to know the answer to the question, too. "So how are you going to avoid broken engagements in the future?"

"Simple." She opened those gorgeous blue eyes and gazed at him. "I'm going to pick the man instead of waiting for the man to pick me. I'm going to take my time about it and make sure it's what *I* want and I'm not just going along with his idea."

"I see."

"I've had a reasonable amount of interest from men."

"I'm sure you have." He massaged her toes, working from the base to the tip, and watched a dreamy expression steal over her face. He should get a medal for not seducing her right now. She was becoming more relaxed by the second, and a relaxed woman was usually a willing woman.

"And that's the problem. I've allowed them to pursue me and catch me. I was never the pursuer, only the pursued. They wanted me, so I convinced myself that I wanted them, too, because I was flattered and it made life easy."

So the poor saps were screwed from the get-go. "Just so you know, I don't want you at all."

Her smile was damn near irresistible. "Yes, you do."

He wanted to kiss her so much his throat ached. "No, I don't. What you see going on is a case of indigestion. Lust and indigestion look remarkably alike, especially in the human male."

"You don't have to pretend indifference, because the thing is, I decided hours ago that I wanted you."

After what she'd just said about choosing her potential husband, he needed some clarification. "How do you mean that, exactly?"

"It's okay for you to want me. It's a mutual attraction. I'm not just going along with what you have in mind. I want what you want."

"We're just talking about sex, right? Not rings and weddings and stuff like that?"

She laughed. "Absolutely! No way am I ready to choose a husband, but I have to start being more proactive with men in general. So to be perfectly clear, we're just talking about sex."

"Which we can't have tonight." Still rubbing her foot with one hand, he slid the other inside her pant leg and caressed her smooth calf.

Her lips parted slightly and her eyes grew unfocused. "True."

He brushed her soft skin with his fingertips. "So I won't be peeling off your jeans and exploring what's under those silk panties."

She swallowed. "How do you know they're silk?"

"Sparkly toes, stylish shoes, designer jeans. They're silk." His cock grew hard.

"Good guess."

"And they're pink." Why he was torturing himself, he wasn't sure.

"Lavender."

"I was close. Trimmed with lace."

Nodding, she met his gaze. "And wet."

He groaned and squeezed his eyes shut. "That was a low blow."

"Yeah." Her voice was husky. "Sorry."

He opened his eyes and looked at her. "I doubt it."

"Okay, I'm not sorry."

"Olivia, we're not going to make out on this couch. I'm not about to have Sarah come to investigate strange noises and discover us writhing around naked on her furniture."

"I'm not, either."

"She's my hostess."

"She's my client."

"Which settles that issue." He withdrew his hand from her pant leg. "Shall we go to bed?"

"We're not doing anything upstairs, either."

"I'm aware of that. But I think we'd be wise to separate before we start something we feel compelled to finish."

"Right."

He gently—and reluctantly—placed her foot back on the leather cushion and stood. "Going upstairs to our separate rooms and closing our respective doors seems like the only solution."

"But first we have to bank the fire and take Rodney out to pee."

He shook his head. "No, *I* have to do those things. I'm the one who said I would. You can go on up."

"I'm not letting you struggle with the dog by yourself. It's still raining."

"Yeah, well, it won't be the first time I've been wet today."

She winked at him. "Me, either."

"Stop it, Olivia."

"Oh, come on, Wyatt. Isn't this kind of exciting? When was the last time you were under the same roof with a woman you wanted and you were forced to restrain yourself?"

He had to think about that. "I try not to get into those kinds of situations," he said at last. "I have to go back to my teenage years for a memory like that."

"Look at it this way. We'll get together eventually, so it'll be that much more fun when we finally accomplish it."

He sighed and levered himself off the couch. "I'm

not sure I agree with that reasoning, but if you're determined to help me deal with Rodney, then I accept the offer. I know a lot more about banking fires than taking dogs out to do their business."

"Like I said, we had dogs while I was growing up. I think my father hoped a dog would keep me from missing a mother quite so much."

"Did it?"

"Probably. But nothing takes the place of having a mother."

"Unless she's my mother."

"Even then. At least she was there."

"Physically, maybe, but—" Wyatt caught himself. He didn't want to talk about his mother any more tonight. "I'll get the fire bedded down for the night. Do you know if Rodney has a leash?"

"I'm sure he does. I'll go see if it's hanging by the front door." She grabbed her shoes and got up. "I'll get him over there while you handle the fire. We can do this." She patted her thigh. "Come, Rodney! That's a good boy."

Wyatt wasn't nearly as confident as Olivia. He'd never dealt with a rain-averse dog and a bedtime potty issue. But if Olivia had grown up in Pittsburgh with dogs, then she had to know about getting them outside in rain, sleet and snow.

After he was satisfied with the condition of the fire he set the screen in front of it. Once he did, the room was considerably darker, so he moved a votive candle to the stone hearth to give them a little light when they came back in. Then he walked over to the entryway where Olivia stood with Rodney on a leash.

Wyatt reached for a yellow slicker hanging on a peg. "Ready to suit up for the rain?"

"I have an idea. How about taking the flashlight and going back to the kitchen to find him a treat?"

"Like what?" He took the flashlight she handed him.

"Something bite-sized that we can give him as a reward. Maybe get a piece of chicken and tear some meat off it. But don't bring a whole chicken piece. They can't handle the bones."

"I know that much. All right. I'll see what I can find." Hanging the slicker back on its hook, he switched on the light and headed toward the dark hallway. At the end of it he passed through a large dining room that Mary Lou had explained was where the hands ate their midday meal.

In the kitchen his lantern was still sitting on a counter, so he turned off the flashlight and switched on his own light. He had the refrigerator door open and the lantern held high when someone tapped him on the shoulder. He jumped and yelled as if he'd been hit with a cattle prod.

When he spun around, he found Mary Lou standing there in a red silk nightgown that he never would have imagined her wearing. He lowered the lantern, although she hadn't looked particularly embarrassed to be caught in a negligee.

"What the hell are you doing, boy? If you're after a midnight snack, then forget about it. We're not supposed to open that refrigerator any more than we have to with the power out."

He felt like a kid caught raiding the cookie jar. Then again, it was kind of a good feeling. As a kid, he'd raided the cookie jar, which had only held bakery cookies, hundreds of times. Nobody had noticed. People around this ranch paid attention. They cared about what went on, and he liked that.

"We have to coax Rodney out to do his business," he said. "Olivia thought we should bring a treat, like a hunk of chicken or something."

"Well, that's easy. Close that refrigerator door and shine the light over on the cupboards to the right of the stove."

Wyatt did as he was told, like any twenty-something guy would do when confronted by a grandma-type giving orders.

"There's a jar of dog treats on the second shelf. Just take a couple of those and you'll be good to go."

"Thanks, Mary Lou." Wyatt found the jar with no trouble, unscrewed the top and took out a couple of bone-shaped biscuits. "Sorry if I woke you."

"You didn't. That damn-fool man Watkins decided to leave his warm bunkhouse and knock on my door. But when I heard someone banging around in my kitchen, I had to investigate. See you in the morning."

"Okay. Thanks again." Wyatt decided not to think about whatever was going on between Mary Lou and Watkins in her apartment. The image might stay burned in his brain forever.

"Oh, and you and Olivia make a cute couple. You should pursue that."

"I...um...she doesn't want to be pursued."

"Hogwash. Any woman likes to be chased after."

"Not this one. She says that was the problem with

her other guys. Now she wants to be the one doing the pursuing."

"Then I guess you'll have to figure out how to get her to chase you until you catch her."

"There's the trick, all right."

"And don't dither around about it. Women like her don't grow on trees, you know."

"I do know." Sticking the dog biscuits in the pocket of his jeans, he turned off the lantern, picked up the flashlight, and made his way back through the dining room and the hallway lined with pictures. He'd known Olivia was special from the moment she'd lowered the window on her Jeep Cherokee. He might not be able to explain exactly why he knew, but he did.

He couldn't say that to her, though. She'd think he was coming on too strong. How ironic that he'd stumbled across a woman he thought might be right for him, and he couldn't go after her or he'd risk ending up like the other three schmucks she'd dumped.

Logically, all three men who had proposed to Olivia might have been ninety-nine percent sure she was the one. But they'd seriously miscalculated. Wyatt cringed at the idea of offering a ring to a woman who later returned it. When he presented a ring to someone, he expected it to stay on her finger for the rest of her life.

He knew from his parents' lives that his preferred scenario wasn't necessarily the norm, but that didn't stop him from being determined that it would be the norm for him. He'd seen marriages that worked for the long-term. He suspected there were some in the Chance family, his mother and Jonathan notwithstanding.

He found Olivia crouched down next to Rodney. She

had rain boots on her feet and a slicker over one arm as she talked earnestly to the dog.

"You need to empty your bladder, Rodney," she said. "It's not good to hold it too long. I've made that mistake a few times when I was working and couldn't take a break. It's not good for you."

Wyatt couldn't help smiling. Olivia might have dumped three guys, but she wasn't without compassion. She would probably argue that leaving them had been an act of kindness because they would have been unhappy in the marriage.

She glanced up. "Did you find some treats?"

"Thanks to Mary Lou, I have a couple of dog biscuits in my pocket."

"She wasn't asleep?"

"No, and please don't ask why. I'd rather forget what I know. In fact, if the Men in Black could come through and zap my memory, I'd be a happy camper."

Olivia giggled. "But you're already a happy camper. Adventure trekking. That's what you do."

"True enough. Ever been camping?" Bracing a hand against the wall, he pulled off one of his boots.

"Nope."

"So you weren't a Girl Scout?" He took off the other boot.

"For a little while, but money was tight and I dropped out."

"I didn't think it was that expensive." Money was one thing Wyatt hadn't worried about when he was growing up.

"It isn't really, but I saw my dad's face when I told him I needed a uniform, and it wasn't worth having him angst over it. Consequently, the only tent I've been in was a blanket draped over a clothesline in the backyard."

"Ever wanted to try camping?" He took the rain boots she handed him and shoved his feet inside.

"Is that an invitation, Mr. Wilderness Guide?"

Play it cool, dude. Let her chase you. "I guess it could be, if you're interested." He stomped his feet to adjust the fit of the rubber boots.

"I'm definitely interested if I can do it with a pro."

He was glad the darkness hid his smile of triumph. "Then we should go camping sometime. Not right away, because I'm hoping Jack will agree to go out with me for a night or two this week, but I'd be happy to take you when we're both free."

"Alone in a tent." She stood. "That could be fun."

He pictured Olivia naked on a down sleeping bag. With great effort, he kept his tone nonchalant. "It definitely has promise."

7

IMAGES OF SEX IN A TENT with Wyatt got Olivia so hot she was eager to go outside and cool off. Without further comment, she put on the yellow slicker and flipped up the hood. "I'm taking the umbrella." She grabbed a collapsible black umbrella leaning in the corner by the door. "If I keep the rain off him, he might be more cooperative."

Wyatt fastened the snaps on his slicker and picked up the flashlight. "I'll bet most dogs go out in the rain no problem."

"Not necessarily. Some dogs love it and some dogs hate it. Just like people." She tucked the umbrella under her arm. "I'll go out first. Give me one of the dog biscuits and I'll coax him down the porch steps."

Pulling up his slicker, Wyatt dug in his pocket and handed her a biscuit. Rodney brightened and wagged his tail.

"See? He wants that treat. If I can tempt him down the steps with the first one, we'll give him the second one as a reward." She opened the door and rain-freshened air cooled her face.

Stepping out on the porch, she crouched down and held out the dog biscuit. "Come on, Rodney. Out the door, big boy."

Nose twitching, Rodney ventured out onto the porch as Olivia backed away toward the steps.

"Smells good out here," Wyatt said as he came out and closed the door behind him. He flicked on the flashlight. "Rain, wet pine needles and smoke."

She paused at the edge of the steps and put up the umbrella. "Rain smells better here than it did in Pittsburgh. Okay, if you could hold this over him as we walk, I'll handle the leash and the treat."

"Sure thing." He took the umbrella, positioned it over the dog and swept the area with the beam of light. "No tree branches in your way."

"Thanks. I'll bet sometimes you camp in the rain."

"Sometimes. It's tricky working with a fire when it's raining, but it can be done."

Watching him in his element would be a turn-on, she thought. Of course, as ramped up as she was right now, just watching him breathe was a turn-on.

But she was here to help the dog, not fantasize about sex with Wyatt. Holding the treat in one hand and the leash in the other, she tugged gently as she edged backward down the first step and into the rain. "That's it, Rodney. Down the steps." The rain fell steadily, but not quite as hard as earlier in the evening. "Wyatt will cover you with the umbrella so you don't get quite so wet."

With painstaking slowness the two of them maneuvered the dog down the steps and onto the gravel.

"My plan is to lead him over to one of those spruce trees," she said.

"All that way?"

"He's a boy. He needs something to lift his leg on."

Wyatt chuckled. "I can see you're determined to do this right."

"It's that or risk an accident in that beautiful house. I'll keep a tight hold on the leash, but if he shows signs of backing up, block him from behind."

"Okay. If I have to, I'll break out some of my old football moves."

"You played?"

"Nearly every sport I could squeeze into my schedule. It got me out of the house. And it was a legitimate way to get sweaty and dirty."

"I was the opposite, an indoor, playing-with-dolls kind of kid. I set up a beauty shop and spent hours on their hair." She waggled the biscuit as she backed across the gravel drive and used the flashlight beam to watch for big puddles. Rodney followed. Although he whined a couple of times in protest, the umbrella seemed to give him a feeling of protection. "I played beauty parlor with the dogs, too."

Wyatt's boots crunched on the gravel as he followed close behind Rodney and sheltered him with the umbrella. "So that's why you became a beautician? Playing beauty salon with your dolls and your dogs?"

"No." She waggled the biscuit again. "I got into it because I practically lived at a salon called A Cut Above. My dad had no idea what to do about my hair and the salon was only a couple of blocks away, so he took me there when I was two. After that I went once a week, sometimes twice, until I graduated from high school. Those women were my substitute moms."

"Now *that* must have been expensive."

"I'm sure they felt sorry for him and gave him a smokin' deal. Plus I started helping out when I was old enough to fold towels and sweep the floor. Then of course I went to work there after I graduated from beauty school."

Talking about A Cut Above always swamped her with nostalgia. For a while the only sounds were the patter of the rain and the soft crunch of their boots on the gravel.

"I'll bet it was hard to leave that place," Wyatt said at last.

"Yes, it was." It was the hardest thing she'd ever done. She'd known some of those women for twenty-five years. But her father's heart had been set on moving to Jackson Hole, and he'd convinced her that they were in a rut living in Pittsburgh. "I still call back there once a week." Glancing behind her, she saw that they'd reached the edge of the gravel. "This part might be harder because of the mud. He won't want to walk through it."

Wyatt gave a resigned sigh. "I already figured that out. If you can hold the umbrella and take over with the flashlight, I'll carry him to the tree."

"All right." She had to hold the umbrella and the biscuit in one hand and the flashlight in the other, but she managed the trade-off.

Leaning down, Wyatt scooped Rodney into his arms. "Oof. You are heavy, dog. I can see why Sarah put you on a diet."

"It's just that his bones are dense, remember?" Olivia

held the umbrella over man and dog as they squished through grass and mud to the nearest spruce.

"It's just because he's porky, is what I'm saying."

"He'll be lighter on the way back."

"He damned well better be." Wyatt lowered him to the ground under the tree. "I don't think you need the umbrella right here. The branches are shielding him."

"You're right." Setting the umbrella on its side on the ground, she offered Rodney the dog biscuit. "Here you go. That's a good boy. Now do your thing."

Rodney chomped happily on the biscuit, swallowed it, and stood looking up at them and wagging his tail.

"Go ahead, Rodney." Olivia made shooing motions with the flashlight beam. "Do your business."

"I swear to God this is turning into a three-act play." Wyatt tossed back his hood and crouched down next to the dog. "Want me to show you how it's done, Rod?"

The dog whined again and licked Wyatt's hand.

Olivia burst out laughing.

"Well, I'm not gonna demonstrate, because there will be no unzipping of flies out here. It could lead to something else."

Olivia nearly choked on her laughter, but a hot river of lust sluiced through her at the thought of Wyatt's potentially unzipped fly. "Honestly."

"Well, it could."

"Not likely, considering the rain and the mud factor."

He rose to his feet and turned to her, his face in shadow. "Then I guess you've never done it up against a tree."

"Uh, no." Her pulse raced. "Can't say that I have."

His voice was low and filled with repressed desire.

"We might have to remedy that if we go camping together."

She wanted him so much she could barely breathe. "Promises, promises."

"Those are the kind I like to make." Dropping the leash to the ground, he anchored it with his boot as he took the flashlight from her and shut it off.

She trembled in anticipation of his next move. "It's dark out here without a flashlight."

"Are you afraid of the dark?" A rustling sound indicated he'd shoved the flashlight in the back pocket of his jeans.

"Not when I'm with a professional wilderness guide." Her heart beat so fast she felt dizzy.

"There you go." He brushed back the hood of her slicker and cradled her head in one large hand.

"Are you going to kiss me?"

"Thinking about it." His tone was lazy, almost casual. "How would you feel about that?"

"I kind of like the idea."

"I sort of do, too." Cupping her damp cheek in his other hand, he settled his mouth firmly over hers.

The fuse had been burning within her for hours. With his deliberate kiss the flame reached the keg of gunpowder, blowing away all thought and leaving only heat and fire. She moaned and wrapped her slicker-clad arms around his neck as her mouth opened in surrender.

He took what he offered, thrusting his tongue inside, mimicking the connection they both wanted, yet were denying themselves. With several loud pops he unfastened the snaps down her front and cupped her breasts in both hands. She pressed against his palms, desperate for his touch.

He lifted his mouth a fraction from hers as he massaged her breasts through her shirt. "The whole time I was rubbing your feet, I really wanted this."

"I wanted this, too. Oh, Wyatt, kiss me. I want your mouth on me."

He kissed her eyes, her cheeks, the tip of her nose. "Where do you want my mouth, Olivia?"

She groaned. "Everywhere. All over. Wyatt..." His name turned into a wail of frustration. "You're torturing me."

His breathing was heavy. "No more than I'm torturing myself. Right now we have to settle for this." He deepened the kiss, ravishing her in a way that left no doubt what he would like to do once they were free to explore each other.

The wind picked up and blew a shower of water down from the pine needles, drenching them. Wyatt just kept kissing her, his mouth supple, wet and intoxicating. She squirmed closer, wanting more, wanting everything.

A series of sharp barks jolted them out of their frenzied kiss. Wyatt let her go. She put her hand to her chest and struggled to remember their original purpose in coming out here. Oh, yes, Rodney.

Leaning down, Wyatt scooped up the end of the leash. Then they both looked at the dog. Rodney had been hit by the same splash of water as they had, but he didn't seem nearly as pleased with the erotic feel of it.

Slowly he lifted his muzzle and began to bay in true hound-dog style.

"No, Rodney!" Olivia dropped to her knees and held his mouth closed. "Don't do that! You'll wake up the whole house!"

"I think he mostly wanted to get our attention."

Olivia glanced up at Wyatt. "Guess that wasn't so easy to do."

"Nope." His grin flashed in the dim light. "You are one great kisser, Sedgewick."

"Speak for yourself, Locke. I'm surprised you didn't create a layer of fog around this spruce tree from all that steam."

His grin softened. "I loved kissing you, Olivia. I could do it all night. And it's going to be hell trying to sleep when that luscious body of yours is right down the hall. But we need to get back to the house and do our damnedest to be respectful houseguests."

"But what about Rodney? We stopped watching him. Now we don't know if he did anything or not."

"You're right, so I'll take him up to my room, which will serve a couple of purposes. If he didn't go just now and ends up peeing on the floor, I'll be the one to clean it up. Also, I won't be tempted to creep down to your room when I know this dog would probably start howling if I did."

"Rodney's a canine chastity belt."

"Something like that." Wyatt lifted up his slicker and fished out the second treat from his pocket. "Here you go, Rod. Sorry about the unexpected shower."

"I'll bet he went, after all. I'd hate to think we did all of this for nothing."

Wyatt's eyebrows lifted. "Nothing?"

"I didn't mean it like that. I just—"

"I'm perfectly willing to let the dog wait in the rain a little longer. I'd hate for you to leave here feeling all let down and disappointed."

She held her breath, wondering if he'd pull her into his arms again. "I don't feel let down and disappointed. I feel keyed up and horny, and if you kiss me again it'll only get worse." And wouldn't that be fun?

But instead he backed off. "Wouldn't want that."

"Right." Oh, yes, she would.

LATER THAT NIGHT, AS WYATT tossed and turned on a mattress built for two, he wondered if he could maintain the facade of coolness with Olivia. Their kisses had raged through him like a brush fire, and every time he thought of the way she'd responded, his cock turned to granite. Instead of sleeping, which was the smart thing to do, the thing Rodney was doing on the braided rug beside Wyatt's bed, he imagined making love to Olivia.

He wondered if she had plans tomorrow. He didn't know a lot about beauticians and salons, but he was reasonably sure that they wouldn't be open on Sunday, especially in a small town like Shoshone. Olivia could have things to do on her day off, though.

Still, she might be willing to spend time with him, and Jack wouldn't be home until late afternoon. As he thought about what they might do together, he admitted to himself that mostly he wanted to get her alone somewhere. Would that be too obvious?

And if he succeeded in working out a way they could be alone, then he needed his stuff from the Bunk and Grub. Specifically, he needed one certain item, something he carried with him, although only God knew why he did. He hadn't had a girlfriend in over a year.

Actually, he did know why he kept condoms on hand and had done it for years. Funny he hadn't figured that out before. His mother hadn't bothered to have any heart-to-heart talks with him except once, and the subject had been birth control.

She'd handed him a box of Trojan condoms, which had embarrassed the hell out of him, but she'd insisted that he listen to what she had to say. A lecture about unplanned pregnancies had followed. She'd emphasized how such a disaster could change someone's life forever.

Now he knew where that lecture had come from. She'd married Jonathan Chance because she'd been pregnant with his child. These days people didn't always believe that a marriage had to follow a pregnancy, but his mother had believed it back then.

Even after only a few hours at the ranch, Wyatt could understand why she'd thought marrying Jonathan was her only option. She'd conceived the heir to the Chance legacy. And when she'd finally made up her mind to leave, she couldn't take that heir with her. Jack belonged here.

She should never have had more children, but he couldn't very well wish she hadn't or he wouldn't exist. But she had not been a good mother, certainly not to Jack, and not to her other boys, either. One lecture about birth control didn't balance out years of indifference. But it had prevented him from making the same mistake she had.

As he lay staring into the darkness, Rodney whined. At Olivia's insistence when they'd started upstairs,

Wyatt had taken the flashlight while she took the votive candle. She'd argued that he had the dog and might need it.

Apparently he did. When he turned it on, Rodney looked for all the world like he had to go outside. Well, crap. Climbing out of bed, he walked to the window. Rain no longer ran in rivulets down the pane, so maybe it had stopped. Maybe Rodney knew that.

"All right, Rod." Wyatt put on his briefs and the jeans and shirt he'd borrowed. No sense in bothering to put on Jack's boots when he was planning to wear the rubber rain boots outside. He left his shirt unsnapped, too. This would be a quick trip.

"At least it better be quick," he told the dog as they left the bedroom, lighting the way with the flashlight. He let Rodney walk to the top of the stairs, but he carried him down because a long flight of steep steps wasn't really Rodney's thing. Once on the ground floor, he put the dog down, and Rodney padded right over to the front door.

"I'll be damned. Okay, let me get some boots on." He abandoned the slicker option, snapped on Rodney's leash and opened the door. Cool air greeted him, soothing his heated skin. Maybe this wasn't such a bad idea after all.

Without coaxing, the basset hound trotted across the porch and made his way down the steps while Wyatt gave him a lit path with the flashlight. Crossing the gravel drive took no time at all. But at the muddy area on the far side of the driveway, Rodney paused.

"I'm not sure how you're going to be a tracking dog if you can't stand mud, my friend." But Wyatt picked him up and transported him over to the tree, where Rodney hiked his leg and did what everybody had been trying for hours to get him to do.

"Feel better, now?"

Rodney yipped his answer.

Wyatt stood under the tree for a moment reliving his encounter with Olivia. His groin stirred. Either they'd find some time alone tomorrow, or he was going to be one frustrated guy. But suggesting a picnic seemed lame, especially when the ground would be wet and muddy after all this rain.

At some point he'd help her get her Jeep out of the ditch, but he couldn't imagine parlaying that into anything cozy. Then inspiration struck. The night breeze must have blown the cobwebs from his brain because he had the perfect solution.

In describing the ranch, his mother had mentioned a sacred Shoshone site a short drive from the house. The marker was a large, flat rock about the size and length of a pickup truck and it was laced with white quartz, a stone that was thought to conduct special energy and sparkled in the sun.

He'd been a little surprised that she'd talk about the site because usually she downplayed the fact that she was half-Shoshone. That made him a quarter Shoshone, though he didn't look the least bit Native American. And he wanted to see this site.

Apparently the tribe didn't visit the spot anymore, even though the Chance family had given them permission to do so whenever they wanted. Times had changed. But many years ago, the rock had been the location for tribal ceremonies. Inviting Olivia to drive out there with him was the perfect excuse to get her alone, and—if he was a very lucky guy—naked.

8

OLIVIA HAD HEARD WYATT go outside with Rodney because, big surprise, she'd been unable to sleep. Most of the clouds had drifted away, leaving the moon and stars to play hide-and-seek behind the ones that were left. Kneeling by her bedroom window and resting her arms on the sill, she watched him move across the gravel. The flashlight bobbed rhythmically as he walked in that loose-hipped way that told her a man knew how to use those hips in bed.

His shirt billowed out, which meant he hadn't bothered to fasten the snaps. She intended to stay here until he walked back. An opportunity to catch a glimpse of his bare chest was worth the wait.

She liked that he hadn't left his shirt open for a calculated macho display of muscles. He thought he was alone with the dog and had no idea she was at the window, her attention glued to his every move.

At the far edge of the drive, he switched off the flashlight, leaned down and scooped Rodney into his arms just as the moon came out from behind a cloud. She had a great view of his buns in the borrowed jeans that were delightfully snug. Ordinarily she'd feel shallow for obsessing about a guy's body like this, except that she also admired the person inside, so ogling didn't seem quite so awful. She admired his cheerful attitude and his courage in coming here and trying to become friends with Jack.

He was risking rejection and she hoped to hell that wasn't going to happen. She didn't know Jack very well. Everybody knew his wife, Josie, because she owned the Spirits and Spurs and still worked there regularly. But Jack spent his time on the ranch, so Olivia had limited knowledge, mostly gained during Emily and Clay's wedding two months ago.

Jack had cut loose a little at the wedding, and people had told her that he'd been quite the party animal in his younger days. But after his dad died he'd retreated into a workaholic shell. Josie and little Archie had brought him out of that shell, apparently, but the whole issue with his mother still affected him. His initial response to Wyatt proved that.

But Wyatt had come back, wearing his heart on his sleeve. She wished she could protect that vulnerable heart somehow, because she wasn't convinced that Jack would be any more cordial than he had been before. Maybe she'd find a reason to hang around tomorrow, if nobody objected, so that she could be there when Jack arrived.

After spending quality time with Rodney in the shadow of the spruce tree, Wyatt emerged carrying the dog again. Damn. That dog was obscuring her view of Wyatt's most excellent pecs and abs. But then he reached the gravel, set Rodney on all fours and straightened.

The moon and clouds were still involved in a dance, but they separated long enough to illuminate Wyatt— divine intervention as far as Olivia was concerned. Her breath caught at the beauty of him. Men weren't supposed to be beautiful, but Wyatt was.

Moonlight painted him in shades of gray, as if he were the subject of an artistic black-and-white photo. Dominique would be able to capture this on film, but Olivia would have to rely on her memory. No problem. She wouldn't soon forget how the light sculpted his contours and added soft smudges of chest hair that formed a blurry line that disappeared beneath the waist-band of his jeans.

Her fingers itched to touch him, but he was out of reach tonight. He would soon be back in his room and right down the hall, but he might as well be on another continent as far as Olivia was concerned. The thought of causing Sarah any embarrassment gave her heart-burn. No matter how much she wanted Wyatt, and that was a whole lot, she wouldn't breach the invisible bar-rier Sarah had erected between the two wings of the upper story.

As Wyatt crossed the gravel drive he glanced up to-ward her window. She doubted he could see her there, but she liked knowing he'd thought of her during his late-night ramble. But she was dead serious about how she'd handle their relationship beyond the initial sexual involvement. If she and Wyatt turned out to be more than friends with benefits, she wanted to make damned sure that it was her idea and not his to take it to the next level.

Wyatt and Rodney reached the porch and disappeared under the roof. The front door creaked open, and the sharp sound of the dog's toenails on the hardwood floor and the softer thud of Wyatt shucking his boots told her they'd soon be trudging up the stairs. She had to talk long and hard to herself to keep from walking out and meeting them at the top of those stairs.

That would accomplish nothing except to frustrate both her and Wyatt even more. Climbing back into bed, she listened for Wyatt's footsteps and knew from his heavy tread that he was carrying the basset hound. It made an endearing mental picture.

Then they reached the second floor, and the dog's nails clicked along the hardwood while Wyatt's progress was virtually silent in his bare feet. How she yearned for him. But she would have to wait. Morning seemed an eternity away.

RODNEY TURNED OUT TO BE a damned fine alarm clock. Before the sun was up, he'd begun pacing the floor and whining as if he had to go out again. Mumbling in protest, Wyatt left his warm bed and started pulling on his borrowed clothes. He hadn't expected to sleep at all, but eventually he'd drifted off.

His dreams had been excellent, filled with a very naked and willing Olivia, and pulling the jeans over his morning wood was not a fun exercise. "You're worse than a new baby, Rod, old chum. I've never had a new baby, but I understand they interrupt your sleep a lot."

Rodney came over and started licking his bare toes.

"And you can knock that off, too, Rod. The only person I want licking my toes is sleeping down the hall. At least I hope she is. I hope everyone on this frickin' ranch is asleep because it's barely light out. This is beyond early, and I know early."

Opening his bedroom door, he staggered out into the hall. Josie appeared coming from the other direction, Archie clutched in her arms. "Gotta deal with the baby," she said in a sleep-roughened voice.

"Gotta deal with the dog." Wyatt let her go down the stairs ahead of him.

"You'll make a good dad, Wyatt," she said over her shoulder.

"I already feel like one, except this guy needs to lose some of this baby fat." With a sigh, he picked up Rodney and carried him down the winding staircase. Then he clipped the leash to his collar and opened the front door.

Although he wasn't overjoyed to be roused out of bed this early after so little sleep, the minute he stepped out on the porch, his weariness vanished. The front of the house faced a spectacular view of the Grand Tetons, still snow-covered as spring moved into summer.

The view had been obscured by rain yesterday, but this morning the pale pink of an impending sunrise bathed the jagged peaks and took Wyatt's breath away. Knowing his mother had walked away from such beauty underscored how different they were.

San Francisco had spectacular views as well, but his mother had never mentioned that as her reason for living there. She'd wanted an urban life and a rich husband. Not that anyone would have called Jonathan Chance a pauper. Any fool could see that the Last Chance was worth a lot of money, but the family would have to sell in order to tap those millions. His mother obviously preferred ready cash.

Accompanying Rodney across the gravel drive to the dog's chosen spruce tree, Wyatt shivered in the morning chill and wished for a jacket. But other than the temperature, it was glorious out here. He savored the scents of pine and wet earth and glanced up as a hawk wheeled overhead.

Just as Rodney finished anointing the tree trunk, Wyatt heard activity down at the barn and several paint horses appeared in the pasture, manes and tails flying as they celebrated their freedom. The barn dogs Olivia had mentioned bounded out and ran up to greet Rodney.

Thanks to leather collars hand-tooled with their names, Wyatt was able to identify them. Butch was a medium-sized dog, a mixed breed with short hair that was mostly tan except for a patch of white on his snub nose. Sundance was slightly smaller with a curly black coat and floppy ears.

All three dogs participated in a round-robin of nose-to-tail greetings, but Butch and Sundance also trotted over to Wyatt seeking attention. Crouching down, he ruffled their coats and scratched behind their ears. "Guess Rod must have vouched for me, huh?"

Panting, the dogs both grinned at him. A whistle from the barn sent them racing back down, probably for their breakfast. Wyatt realized he was smiling. He could easily lose his heart to this ranch and the surrounding countryside. And that wasn't even taking into account the woman he'd kissed last night under this very tree.

Rodney started back toward the house, obviously

interested in his next meal, too. Wyatt was attached to Rodney by the nylon leash but the dog was far more eager to go in than Wyatt was. The rockers lining the porch were still wet, but he could imagine coming out here with a cup of coffee and just…appreciating. No doubt that's why the chairs were there.

The minute he walked through the front door he caught the scent of coffee and wondered how someone was accomplishing that if the power was still off. But if there was coffee in the making, he'd sure like to find a towel and wipe off one of those rockers.

He wasn't sure where his boundaries lay, though. Sarah had insisted that he stay here, but that didn't mean he could act as if he owned the place. He had to be very careful about that, in fact.

Rodney, on the other hand, had no such hang-ups. Once Wyatt unhooked the leash from his collar he trotted down the hall toward the kitchen as if the Last Chance had been built expressly for his comfort. Wyatt followed him, figuring the dog gave him an excuse to investigate what was happening in the kitchen.

In the early morning light he could see the pictures on the wall, but he wouldn't know most of the people. He needed that guided tour Mary Lou had promised him. He also needed coffee.

He found more people in the kitchen than he would have imagined this early. Josie had Archie in his carrier on the table and was rocking him gently while she sipped from a steaming mug. Mary Lou, wearing a fluffy white bathrobe, also sat at the table cradling a mug, and the third person was a fully dressed middle-aged cowboy with a handlebar mustache. He had coffee, too.

"Hi, there, Wyatt!" Mary Lou smiled at him. "Want coffee?"

"Yes, but what kind of magic did you use to make it?"

"Cowboy magic." She glanced at the man sitting next to her at the table. "Watkins, I'd like you to meet Wyatt Locke, Jack's half brother."

Watkins shoved back his chair, stood and extended his hand across the table. "Pleased to meet you, Wyatt."

"Same here, Mr. Watkins." Wyatt shook the cowboy's hand and kept his expression carefully neutral. So this was the "old fool" Mary Lou had no intention of marrying, the same guy who'd knocked on her door in the rain and caught her wearing, probably not by accident, a red negligee.

"Just Watkins, son. That's all I go by. Coffee's in that big thermos over there. Take as much as you want. I'm about to head down to the bunkhouse and reload it."

"Thanks." Wyatt walked over to the counter where a large carafe stood.

"Mugs are in the cupboard above," Mary Lou said. "Need cream? I hope not, because we're limiting how often we open the refrigerator."

"I don't use cream, thanks." Wyatt took down a plain white mug, stuck it under the spigot and pushed on the top of the carafe. A stream of dark, fragrant coffee poured out. Heaven.

When he was finished, Watkins came over and lifted the carafe. "Yep, nearly empty. I'll be back."

"Thanks, Watkins," Josie said. "You're a lifesaver."

"It's the hands who get the credit. They weren't about to go without their coffee this morning."

"So what did they do?" Wyatt asked.

"Hauled out the old campfire coffeepot and turned on the propane barbecue grill," Watkins said. "They'll be cooking bacon and eggs soon. I'll bring some of those up when they're ready."

Wyatt grinned. "Exactly what I would have done. In fact, I didn't even think about the little camp stove I have in the back of my truck. Should I get that out?"

Watkins smoothed his mustache. "Thanks, but I think we've got it covered. They're having fun, as a matter of fact. It'll be their pleasure to feed the ladies. Well, and you, of course. Be right back." Carrying the carafe, he left the kitchen by the back door.

"Look at that Rodney," Mary Lou said. "Waiting so patiently for his breakfast. At least we don't have to cook that." She stood and walked back to the laundry room. "Come on, boy."

Rodney covered the same distance faster than Wyatt would have thought possible on such short legs. "That was a popular suggestion, Mary Lou."

"He loves his food, which is why he's got love handles."

Josie glanced up at Wyatt. "Have a seat, cowboy."

"Oh, I'm not a cowboy." But he pulled out a chair and sat at the oak kitchen table anyway.

"Hey, you wear the clothes, you soon get the attitude. We've seen that happen before, right, Mary Lou?"

Mary Lou chuckled as she returned to her seat at the table. "We certainly have. Your brother Alex, for example. Oh, and Logan Carswell."

Wyatt recognized the name. "Logan Carswell? You don't mean the former catcher for the Cubs."

"One and the same." Mary Lou sounded proud of the fact. "He and Alex were best friends growing up in Chicago, so he came out for Alex and Tyler's wedding last summer, fresh from forced retirement. He turned into a darned good cowboy, don't you think, Josie?"

Josie laughed. "He's so hooked on the cowboy life-style that he had to go to Casper with the rest of the guys even though he doesn't own any horses and doesn't ride competitively, either. But he couldn't stand to be left out. His wife, Caro, would be here tonight but she needed to spend time with her grandmother in Jackson this weekend."

"Huh. Logan Carswell." Wyatt sipped his coffee. The ranch was full of surprises.

Josie eyed him across the table. "You and Olivia seemed to hit it off."

Startled, he met her gaze. Welcome to the other side of this cozy family situation. People felt free to give advice and commentary.

Josie looked amused. "If you'd rather not talk about it, that's okay. Around here we have a bad habit of poking our noses where they don't belong."

"I told him last night that he should stake his claim," Mary Lou said.

Wyatt decided to use the system to his advantage and find out more about Olivia. "Does she date much?"

"No." Josie reached over and started rocking Archie again when he began to fuss. "I think after breaking off three engagements she's turned over a new leaf and is getting choosier."

"She told me about the three engagements," Wyatt said. "And about being more in charge of her love life from now on."

Josie continued to rock Archie's carrier. "Did she tell you why she broke those engagements?"

"Just that it didn't work out."

"Each of those bozos managed, eventually, to make a disparaging remark about her father."

"Oh." That put a new light on the situation. No wonder Olivia wanted to make the choice next time. "He sounds like he's...different."

"He is, and she'll be the first to say it, but woe unto anyone else who pokes fun at him. I find that kind of loyalty admirable."

Wyatt nodded. "So do I. Thanks for telling me."

"Consequently, I don't think she's planning to rush into another engagement any time soon."

"Rushing into an engagement is a bad idea, anyway," Wyatt said. "I want to be pretty damned sure when I ask somebody to marry me."

Mary Lou gazed at him over the rim of her mug. "Sounds like you've never taken that plunge."

"Nope. Like I said, I want to be really, really sure before I drop to one knee in front of a woman." When neither of them responded, he raised his eyebrows. "You don't agree with that?"

"I don't know if you can ever be that sure," Josie said. "You can be crazy about somebody, but there's still a big risk involved. Sometimes you have to be willing to leap and hope the net will appear."

"Or you can be like me." Mary Lou set down her empty mug. "I had your attitude about marriage. Still do, actually. Can't see any reason for it, so here I am, still single at fifty-two."

Josie gave her a nudge. "Watkins would take care of that issue for you in a heartbeat."

"Watkins." Mary Lou blew out a breath.

"Did you call my name, Lulu?" Watkins came through the back door without knocking, a testament to the freedom Mary Lou allowed him in her domain.

She sniffed. "I told you not to call me that."

"Then I'll call you sweetie pie." He held the coffee carafe in one hand and a metal container covered in foil in the other. "Time to break out the chafing dishes. I'm bringing home the bacon."

"I smell coffee and I smell food!" Olivia's cheery voice preceded her as she walked into the kitchen. "Good morning, everyone!"

Wyatt stood up so fast he had to steady his chair to keep it from falling over. Wow, did she look great. She'd tied her hair up in some kind of sassy ponytail that made her look about sixteen, and the impression was enhanced by her bare feet, jeans rolled at the cuffs, and a light green T-shirt with the words Nail Techs Do It with Polish on the front.

As far as he was concerned, she could do it any way she cared to, if she promised to do it with him.

9

THE AROMA OF COFFEE HAD finally drifted up to the second floor, which had roused Olivia out of a very erotic dream involving a certain Wyatt Locke. Knowing a sexy guy like Wyatt was around certainly could cause a girl to rush through her morning ablutions. Cold water could do that, too, and she'd danced her way through a freezing shower.

At least her skin would look pink and healthy after that onslaught. But the hair dryer she'd brought wouldn't work, which had meant towel-drying her hair, which wasn't the optimal method for fluff. She'd wanted to look cute for him, so she'd taken a little extra time to create a bouncy ponytail. A light application of makeup and she'd been good to go.

Her outfit couldn't be changed. She'd brought something fun to wear, thinking she'd just be hanging out with the girls until she went home this morning. She had, however, forgotten to bring another pair of shoes, and the heels just didn't go with her casual clothes. She'd opted for no shoes at all, figuring she could borrow the same rain boots she'd worn before if she needed to go outside.

She'd heard Wyatt's voice as she'd walked down the hallway that led through the dining room and into the kitchen, and that soft baritone had jump-started her pulse rate. By the time she'd arrived she'd been slightly out of breath, strictly from nerves. The size of her crush on him was growing by leaps and bounds.

His smile when he saw her was encouraging, and the light in his gray eyes was even more encouraging. He hadn't shaved yet and she enjoyed the fact that he had a beard going on. There was an intimacy involved in knowing this was the Wyatt she'd see in the morning if they spent the night together in a tent.

She shouldn't be entertaining such thoughts while they were in a crowd of people, though, a crowd that grew larger by the moment as Morgan showed up with SB, followed by Tyler, Emily and Dominique.

Then Sarah and Pam walked in and Sarah immediately took charge of the situation. "Time to move into the family dining room for breakfast."

Olivia had never seen the room Sarah referred to. The main dining room with its four round tables that could each accommodate eight people didn't seem like the right venue for a family meal. Instead Sarah led everyone through double doors that Olivia hadn't noticed before. Then she hit the light switch and muttered a soft curse.

"That's okay," Mary Lou said. "I can fix this." Shortly she returned with a candelabra, each taper lit. "Voilà."

"Breakfast by candlelight," Emily said. "I love it. I'll have to try that with Clay after he gets home."

Olivia was entranced. The flickering candles revealed a table perfectly sized for the number of guests eating breakfast. In no time Sarah, Pam and Mary Lou had everyone set with dishes, utensils and cloth napkins, all matching.

The food arrived in shifts, and Olivia soon realized that the hands down at the bunkhouse were cooking on the barbecue grill. She recognized Watkins, Mary Lou's sweetheart, as the delivery man. The meal was chaotic, fun, and somehow she ended up sitting next to Wyatt.

His knee touched hers under the table, and when he didn't move it, she decided he'd meant to do that. The point of contact felt warm and sent squiggles of awareness through the rest of her.

Wyatt unfolded his napkin and laid it in his lap before glancing over at her. "How did you sleep?"

It could have been an innocent question, a simple conversation-starter, but she knew it wasn't. "Fine."

"Really?" He sounded disappointed.

"You didn't want me to sleep well?" She couldn't keep the teasing note out of her voice.

"Well, yeah, of course I wanted you to sleep well. I'm glad you did. That's great." He passed her a platter of scrambled eggs. "Want some eggs?"

"Thanks." She started to take it from him.

"Go ahead and dish yourself. I'll hold it for you."

"Okay." She took a couple of spoonfuls. Apparently lust made her hungry, because she could hardly wait to tuck into the food.

The bacon came around next, followed by hash

browns and then toast. Each time Wyatt repeated his gallant gesture of holding the platter while she loaded her plate. He was so cute. She had the strongest urge to lean over and kiss him on his bristly cheek, but that wasn't appropriate in front of all these people, even in the subdued light of candles.

Conversation flowed around the table. Most of it had to do with family matters that didn't concern them, so after the food was all served Olivia and Wyatt were free to continue where they'd left off.

"I trust you slept well, too," she said.

He chewed and swallowed a bite of toast. "Like a baby. Didn't move all night long."

She lowered her voice. "I know that's not true. You took Rodney outside again."

"And how would you happen to know that?"

"I watched you walk him over to the spruce tree."

"Hmm." He didn't look at her, but his cheek creased in a smile. "That was a couple of hours after you went to bed, Olivia."

"So, maybe I didn't sleep quite *that* soundly."

He continued to eat without looking at her. "I guess not. I was pretty quiet going downstairs."

"The stairs creak."

"Not much." He concentrated on his meal for a few moments. "So you heard me go downstairs and went over to the window? Is that what you're saying?"

"I was just curious."

"And awake."

"Maybe."

"Too bad you didn't slip on a bathrobe and come out

there with me. It was nice. A half moon, some stars, a few stray clouds, the sound of a dog tinkling…"

Fortunately she didn't have a mouthful of food when he said that or things would have turned ugly. As it was she got the giggles and had to use her napkin to wipe her eyes.

"What's so funny over there?" Dominique asked.

"Rodney," Olivia said between fits of laughter.

"Rodney's in the dining room?" Sarah glanced around. "We need to move him out of here, then. We're trying to break him of begging, but it's slow going."

"Rodney's not in here," Mary Lou said. "I made sure he was in his bed asleep in the kitchen before we all came in. I think he had a hard night."

"Yeah, how did that go?" Tyler asked. "We could *not* get that dog to go outside in the rain. He was like this immovable object."

"They used dog treats," Mary Lou said. "Right, Wyatt?"

Tyler smacked her forehead. "Brilliant. So he went, then?"

"Uh, no," Wyatt said. "We got him out there, but he didn't go. At least I don't think he did."

Olivia did her best to look nonchalant during Wyatt's explanation and hoped to hell nobody could tell from her expression that some hanky-panky took place under that spruce tree.

"I took him up to my room so I could keep an eye on him," Wyatt continued. "A couple of hours later, he started pacing, so I took him out again. This time the rain had stopped, so we had liftoff. Or 'lift-up,' I guess you'd say."

"I can see why Olivia was so entertained." Dominique grinned at him. "You're a funny guy, Wyatt. I'm glad you decided to pay us a visit."

"Me too," he said. "And I apologize for the scruff at the breakfast table. I took Rod out first thing and then was lured into the kitchen by the smell of coffee so a razor blade never made it into the mix."

"Hey," Tyler said. "Without hot water, this girl is not getting in the shower, so you can be as scruffy as you want to be, dude. I won't complain."

Sarah beamed at him. "Besides, anyone who's been that dedicated to my dog's bathroom needs is not going to get a lecture from me about appearing with whiskers at the breakfast table. Thank you, Wyatt."

"Anytime." He drank the last of his coffee. "But I'm starting to feel like the hobo who appears at the back door for a handout, so if you'll all excuse me..."

"The water will be cold," Tyler said. "I know you're a wilderness guide and all that, but if you want my advice, you'll wait for the power to come back on."

"I don't mind cold showers." He pushed back his chair. "Oh, wait. My shaving kit's over at the Bunk and Grub."

Sarah waved a hand dismissively. "No problem. I'm sure there's a pack of disposables and a can of shaving cream in the bathroom next to your bedroom. Just use what you need. But I agree with Tyler. Wait until the power's back on."

"But there's no predicting when that will be, right?"

"No," Sarah admitted.

"Then I'll take my chances with the cold water."

"If you must, you must, then. I can't remember what

else is up there, but I've tried to keep travel-sized toiletries in that bathroom for whoever's staying in that wing. Help yourself."

"I appreciate it." He paused. "I, um, heard there's a sacred Shoshone site on the ranch. I'd like to go see it this morning, if that's okay."

"Of course it's okay," Sarah said immediately. "That's part of your heritage, after all. It's easy to find, but if you'd like somebody to go with you…"

"I'm sure I can find it." Then he turned to Olivia. "Have you been there?"

She wasn't prepared for a direct question and stumbled over her answer. "No, but I thought…I mean, that's really only for…I've never been invited to go, so I—"

"For heaven's sake, go, both of you," Sarah said. "It's a lovely spot, and you should see it, Olivia. We haven't opened it up to tourists and never will, but friends of the family are definitely free to go out there. I think that's a great idea."

"Good." Wyatt pushed back his chair and stood. "I can use my truck to pull Olivia's Jeep out of the ditch after we get back. That'll give the sun a chance to dry up some of the mud."

"No rush." Coffee mug in hand, Sarah relaxed against her chair. "Unless you have plans, Olivia, you're welcome to stay as long as you want."

"What a lovely offer." Sarah's warm welcome felt good, very good. "All I have is chores at home. Well, and checking on my dad. But I'm off tomorrow, too, so I have leeway."

"Speaking of chores," Wyatt said. "I'll help with the

dishes before I get cleaned up. With the power out, there's no dishwasher."

As if in direct response to his comment, the hammered metal chandelier lit up. Everyone cheered and clapped for the return of life as they knew it.

Olivia was happy that no one else would have to take cold showers like the one she'd endured, and that the dishwasher could take care of the breakfast dishes. Electricity was a good thing. But she'd enjoyed doing without it since yesterday.

With candles and a fire the evening had been more romantic. And she agreed with Emily that breakfast by candlelight was an awesome idea. Wyatt seemed like the perfect guy to share those things with, too.

ONCE WYATT KNEW THAT supplies had been left in the upstairs bathroom in what was essentially the guys' wing, he decided to do a thorough search. Maybe he wouldn't find what he was looking for, but then again, someone might have left a box behind.

In the cupboard under the sink he hit pay dirt, a box with six foil packages inside. They were even the brand he normally bought. If he took two, he'd replace them later.

Maybe this was a forgotten box that would never be used. But if some guy had left them here thinking he'd have a stash for a future event, Wyatt didn't want to leave him in the lurch. These had been available when Wyatt desperately needed them and he'd pay it forward.

He wasted no time showering and shaving, although from now on every time he used a razor he'd mourn for that perpetually sharp blade Olivia's dad had invented.

Some might say her father shouldn't have sold out, that if he'd persisted in bringing his blade to market, he would have contributed to the advance of civilization.

Wyatt couldn't fault the guy for the way he'd handled things. Economics was Rafe's department, not Wyatt's. For all he knew, a perpetually sharp razor blade might cause companies to fold and stocks to plummet.

Then there was the selfish part of the equation. The money from the sale of that invention had financed Olivia and her father's move to Shoshone. That action had put her, literally, in Wyatt's path. He wasn't about to criticize her father for selling out.

He wasn't about to criticize her father for anything now that he knew how sensitive she was about her eccentric dad. Wyatt wondered if it bothered her that he was far less loyal to his parents, especially his mother. Surely the commitment level of the parent factored into a child's loyalty.

From what he'd gathered, Olivia's father had been completely committed to Olivia, which was why he'd hustled her off to a beauty salon when he'd recognized his shortcomings in the matter of hairstyling. That whole story touched Wyatt's heart, from the initial tragedy of losing Olivia's mother to the warmhearted beauticians who had welcomed a motherless little girl into their midst.

Olivia's story was nothing like his, and although she'd lost her mother, she'd had buckets full of love to compensate for that loss. He'd had...not much. His father had worked long hours in an attempt to keep up with his wife's spending. Any free time had been split between his sons and the endless demands of a narcissistic wife. Rafe and Wyatt had come out on the short end of the stick.

Harlan Locke had done the best he could but Rafe and Wyatt had basically been on their own. That's what he wanted Jack to understand, once he could talk to him in a neutral setting, maybe around a campfire. Wyatt had great hopes for a camping trip with his half brother.

But Jack wouldn't be home until the end of the day, and Wyatt had plans for the hours between now and then. Putting on another pair of Jack's jeans and a black Western shirt, he thought again about how right the clothes felt. Even the boots fit, which was an unusual coincidence.

But after he and Olivia visited the sacred site he'd make a quick trip over to the Bunk and Grub for his clothes. Whistling, he descended the stairs and found Olivia sitting in the living room waiting for him. No one else seemed to be around.

She stood and walked toward him, her ponytail swaying and rain boots on her feet. She held out a gray felt cowboy hat. "Sarah wanted you to borrow this. She tried to get me to take one, but a hat won't work with the way I did my hair."

"I have a baseball cap in my truck. You could pull your ponytail through the hole in the back."

She made a face. "Then I'll end up with hat hair. I'm not really a hat sort of person."

"Suit yourself." He smiled at her as he took the hat. "It's your nose, so it's up to you if it gets sunburned."

"Won't happen. My makeup is SPF 45."

Personally he thought the baseball cap was a more reliable option, but he knew all about choosing appearance over practicality. His mother did it constantly. Fortunately he recognized that sharing a single trait didn't make Olivia like his mother. Olivia's every action proved that she was not a self-centered egotist.

"Sarah drew me a map." Olivia patted her jeans pocket. "She said the road will be muddy, but your truck should make it fine." She gazed up at him with those incredible blue eyes. "I'm honored that you're taking me out there, Wyatt."

He thought of the foil packages he'd brought along and felt guilty. If she was thinking of this as a spiritual experience and he was focused totally on sex, that would be bad. "Um, I need to confess something." He cleared his throat. "I do want to see the site, but the main reason I suggested the trip is so that we—"

"I know that."

"You do?" He wasn't sounding particularly intelligent.

"Of course. Last night we were ready to rip each other's clothes off. Unless you've had a change of heart, we're both still in that mode."

He sighed in relief. "I haven't had a change of heart. And there was a box of condoms in the upstairs bathroom."

"Oh!" Her eyes widened.

"Did I shock you?"

"No." She moistened her lips. "But you sure as hell ramped up the excitement level for this trip."

He settled the hat on his head. "Then let's take off, little lady."

She laughed. "You really do look like a cowboy, Wyatt."

"I'll take that as a compliment."

"It was meant that way. My dad romanticized the West so much that I've always had a thing for cowboys."

He'd gathered as much the night before, and now she'd admitted it. "You realize once I get my stuff from the Bunk and Grub I'll be wearing boring old hiking clothes again. I could lose all my appeal."

"Unless you take another approach."

"I'd rather not spend the rest of the day shopping for cowboy duds, if that's what you have in mind."

"Nope, that's not what I meant." Her eyes held a mischievous gleam.

"What, then?"

"I'm thinking you might want to just forget about the clothes entirely. Go with the natural look."

"Oh." White-hot lust shot through him. He grabbed her by the hand. "Come on. Let's get the hell out of here." With every moment he spent with Olivia, she became more perfect for him. He just couldn't let her know that.

10

As Olivia rode shotgun in Wyatt's truck for the second time in two days, she thought about how everything had changed since the first time they'd shared the cab of a truck. She couldn't remember ever getting sexual with a guy so soon after meeting him, but getting sexual didn't mean they were headed for the altar. She'd made that clear, at least.

No question that Wyatt had to be the yummiest guy she'd ever run across, though. He was clean-shaven again and had that mint scent going on. When he'd put on the cowboy hat she'd nearly swooned with lust.

"Want the windows down or up?" Wyatt asked.

"Down is fine."

"Good." He lowered both windows with the buttons on the driver's side. "Didn't want to cause a hair issue with the wind."

"I'm not *that* focused on my hair. I just don't like hats."

"Or hat hair," he said with a grin.

"I'm a beautician. I practically grew up in a salon. I think about these things."

"I know. I'm just teasing you. You agreed to go camping with me sometime, so I know you can't be totally a girly-girl."

"I'm pretty much a girly-girl, but I realize I'm not in Pittsburgh anymore."

"So what was so important about moving out here for your dad, anyway? It sounds like Pittsburgh was home."

"It was, but my dad loves old Western movies, has a whole library of them. From the time I was a little kid, he always said if he ever came into money he'd move out to Jackson Hole, Wyoming. So the money arrived and here we are."

"And is he happy with the move?"

"Delirious." Olivia smiled fondly as she thought about how happy her father was these days. "When he's not working in his lab, he sits out on his front porch swing and stares at the mountains."

"What about the cowboy thing? Did he take up riding or get all duded up?"

"No. Says he's too old to start learning to ride and he really doesn't care about clothes. Trust me on that one. Just being here seems to be enough." She glanced over at him. "Why?"

"I'm sort of fascinated by his story, I guess. And if this is what he wanted, I'm glad his razor blade invention gave it to him. I'm also glad he talked you into coming along."

"Once I knew he was completely serious, I couldn't imagine sending him out here by himself. Besides, as I said, he'd watched cowboy movies for all those years, so for me, cowboys were heroes."

"So you came out to find yourself a cowboy?"

"Not exactly. Maybe more to window-shop."

"How's that working out for you?"

She reached over and ran a hand over his denim-covered thigh, causing the muscles to contract under her palm.

He sucked in a breath.

"So far, so good." Wow, he was pure dynamite. Touching him sent flames licking through her.

"Better cut that out if you want to actually make it to the sacred site." His voice roughened. "I've already got sex on the brain."

"I have sex on the brain, too." She gave his thigh a squeeze and moved her hand. "But I want to see the sacred site. It was mentioned when I was here for Emily and Clay's wedding, and I've been curious ever since."

"Then we'll definitely see that site before we get naked, but I'm warning you, I do intend for us to get naked. I have a bed in the back of this truck and I know how to use it."

Olivia's laugh was a little breathless. "I hadn't really thought about where we'd do the deed."

"Believe me, I have."

"Do you even care about the sacred site?" She was fast losing interest, herself.

"Sure I do, but given a choice between admiring the sacred site and admiring your naked body, I'd ditch the site in a second."

"Fortunately we don't have to choose. We're not on a timetable so I think we have a couple of hours to mess around out here, which can include viewing the site and…other things."

"Which is very lucky, because if for some reason

we're thwarted and *don't* have sex, I'm going to have to find another outlet for my frustration. Maybe I can chop a few cords of wood for Sarah."

"A cord is a lot of wood. I've learned that since living here."

"I know how much it is. I'm not exaggerating. If I can't get you naked soon, I'm liable to turn into freaking Paul Bunyan, only instead of having a blue ox, I'll have blue—"

"I get the picture." Dominique was right. Wyatt was extremely entertaining, besides being sexy as hell. "Maybe we have to just do it so you won't turn into a wood-chopping maniac. It might be my civic duty to make sure you're sexually satisfied before we drive back to the ranch."

"That's what I'm saying. I barely slept last night, and here's the kicker—I wasn't slightly interested in relieving the pressure on my own. Usually that's a reasonable option when I'm hot and bothered, but I didn't just want a climax. I wanted you."

"Same here," she said softly.

"Yeah?"

"Yeah, and I don't know what that's all about. We've only known each other since yesterday. That's crazy."

"Probably just hormones."

She nodded. "Or the phase of the moon."

"Or my cowboy outfit."

"Well, there's that. Maybe you should leave the hat on while we do it."

Wyatt smiled. "Whatever it takes, Olivia. Whatever it takes."

She didn't think it would take much, and the hat really wasn't necessary. Wyatt was hot no matter what he wore, or didn't wear.

WYATT WAS RELIEVED THAT his questions about Olivia's father hadn't aroused her suspicion. Now that he knew what had tanked her other relationships, he wondered how weird her dad actually was. But any man who had tried so valiantly to be a good father had earned Wyatt's respect before they even came face-to-face—if they ever did. Given the stakes, Wyatt felt somewhat nervous about that prospect.

But he wouldn't worry about that now because he'd been telling the truth about his lust level. Her hand on his thigh had topped it off nicely, and now he was at full capacity, the needle veering steadily toward the red zone.

He checked the truck's odometer. "We should be getting close according to the mileage on that map Sarah drew for you."

"It's off to the right, she said, and doesn't stick up very far. We're looking for a gray, flat rock." Olivia gazed out through the windshield. "I think that could be it, up ahead." Leaning forward, she put both hands on the dash. "Yep, I think so. Pull over."

He didn't need to be told twice. There was a spot on the side of the road that had been cleared of vegetation. Ruts made by previous vehicles still held some water, so he eased the truck over carefully, loathe to get stuck out here after claiming he could make it out and back on his own.

Once he was off the road he killed the engine. Ahead lay an impressive slab of granite that stuck out of the ground a foot or more. There were no markers, but he hadn't expected any. The Chance family and the Shoshones before them had wanted to keep this area on the down low.

"Let's get out." Olivia unsnapped her seat belt. "From what I heard during the wedding, you're supposed to stand on it to get the full effect."

"I tried to get my mother to tell me what this rock was all about, but she said it was stupid superstition. She's not particularly in touch with her Native American side."

"It has to do with the veins of white quartz running through the granite." Olivia opened her door. "They're supposed to give you mental clarity."

"Hang on. It's muddy out there. Let me come around and help you out."

"I'll be careful." She started down.

So much for gallantry. But at least she had on the rubber rain boots this time. He, on the other hand, was wearing Jack's old boots, and he didn't want to ruin them. Unfastening his seat belt, he opened his door and stepped down, looking for whatever footing he could find where he wouldn't sink ankle-deep.

"Wyatt, you have to come and see this!"

He glanced over and discovered she'd already made it to the rock. Sitting on the edge of it, she pulled off her boots and left them sitting in the mud as she swung herself up on the granite slab and walked barefoot to its center. "I love it," she said. "This is a special place. I can feel it."

He wasn't sure if he loved the site or not, but he loved watching her standing there, feet spread, toes flexing against the smooth stone. She might have spent most of her life in beauty salons, but she would adapt to the outdoors. He sensed an adventurer's spirit in her.

But he'd be wise not to comment on that, either, in case she'd think he was trying to mold her into his perfect companion. Funny, but he'd always imagined he'd end up with a fellow hiker, someone who already owned boots with a serious tread and a GPS. Instead he was weaving fantasies about a beautician who'd never been camping in her life.

He chose a route over to the rock that would minimize the amount of mud he'd get on the boots. In retrospect, he should have worn the pair of rain boots he'd used last night. But they didn't look as cool as Jack's cowboy boots, and now that he knew Olivia's weakness for cowboys, he couldn't help wanting to fit the image.

"Just a suggestion," she said as he approached, "but I would sit on the edge and take off my boots, if I were you. And your socks, too. I think the way to experience this rock is barefoot."

"You're experiencing something?" He agreed there was no point in tracking mud on the weather-polished surface of the rock, which had recently been washed clean by rain, so he sat on the edge and took his boots and socks off, as she'd suggested.

"Yeah," she said softly. "I am. I feel…lighter."

Swinging around to face her, Wyatt got to his feet. He'd heard the theory that certain rocks transmitted energy, and he couldn't deny that in the iron-rich red rocks of Utah and Arizona he'd felt something vibrant in the air. Some of his clients wouldn't hike in those areas. They said the red rock agitated them too much.

This was different, though. The rock felt cool and soothing under his feet as he walked toward her. A gentle sense of peace flowed through him and he let out his breath in an easy sigh.

"Look at how it sparkles in the sun." Olivia pointed to the veins of white quartz running like zebra stripes through the granite.

As Wyatt's glance roamed the surface of the rock, the quartz glittered beneath his feet. "That's kind of pretty."

She held out her hand. "Come closer."

When he touched her warm skin, something flowed between them, a light current that pulsed through his system, making him aware of his surroundings as if he'd never quite seen them before. The green of the trees seemed richer and the blue of the sky grew more intense.

He picked up the scent of wildflowers just beginning to bloom and the quiet drone of bees. He was hyper-aware of Olivia watching him, her pink lips parted, her blue eyes filled with wonder. He heard her soft breathing and found himself matching that rhythm.

He didn't realize that he'd gradually closed the distance between them until she lifted her face to his and all he had to do was lean down for his lips to touch hers in a slow, easy kiss. Nothing in his life had ever been this innocent, this sweet. His breath caught.

Pictures flitted through his mind—Olivia walking down an aisle strewn with flowers, Olivia laughing on a beach somewhere, Olivia cradling a newborn baby. Lifting his head, he looked into her eyes and saw his future. He opened his mouth to tell her.

But then, even though the gauzy pictures lingered

in his mind, he remembered. If that future was to become reality, he couldn't go after it. He couldn't pursue the dreams that tempted him so. He had to let them come to him.

"Come back to the truck with me." His voice was rusty with emotion. "I need you."

"I need you, too."

That was all he had to hear. Swinging her up in his arms, he carried her back across the smooth rock. He stepped into the mud, not caring, and took her to the back of the camper.

He was forced to set her on her feet in the mud while he opened the back window and let down the tailgate. Then she climbed in and he climbed after her, muddy feet and all. Nothing mattered but the fever in his veins and the hope that if he made this ultimate connection with her, the wispy images that had taunted him as they stood on the rock would gain form and substance, would have a chance to become reality.

She started taking off her clothes. Thank God she was as eager for this as he was, because undressing her in the cramped quarters would have been a challenge. Although he'd insinuated that he knew how to use his camper as a seduction site, he never had. He'd only slept solo back here.

Tents were infinitely better for making love, but desperate times called for desperate measures, and she seemed to understand that. Sitting on the quilt covering his double mattress in the back of his truck, she pulled off her T-shirt and unhooked her bra.

He yanked open his shirt and wrenched it off before sitting on the tailgate to get out of his jeans and his briefs. He stuffed his clothes in a corner after extracting the all-important condom from his pocket. Then he set his borrowed hat on top of the balled-up jeans.

"You're not going to wear it?"

He gazed into the dim light of the camper's interior. She was stretched out on the quilt, propped up on one elbow, every scrap of clothing gone. His heart thudded wildly in his chest. She was…incredible.

He had to clear the emotion from his throat before he could speak. "The condom, yes. The hat, no. If I have to wear a Stetson to make an impression on you, then I obviously need some lessons in how to please a woman."

"You're right. It would only get in the way."

"Exactly." Tearing open the condom package, he took care of that chore so he could concentrate all his attention on her. He happened to be down by her feet, so he decided to start there. "You got a little muddy."

"I don't care."

"I can fix that." Using a corner of the quilt, he wiped the mud from her feet. Then he kissed each sparkly toe before moving to her ankles. Such sexy ankles. Lifting each one, he paid homage to it with his mouth and his tongue.

She moaned and arched against the quilt. "How long…before you get…to the good stuff?"

"It's all good stuff." He traced the curve of each calf with his tongue and angled her leg to reach the backs of her knees.

"But I want—" She gasped as he kissed the inside of her thighs, drawing ever nearer to his ultimate destination.

"I know." He blew softly on her moist curls. Light

brown. Now he knew what color her hair *really* was. "But didn't you say anticipation made it better?"

"No fair using that against me."

Sliding up the smooth length of her body, he looked into her eyes. "I promise never to use anything against you. That's not what friends do."

"Wyatt." She cupped his face in both hands. "When we were standing on the rock, did you...was there a feeling of...?" Her uncertain gaze searched his.

"Don't analyze it, Olivia." He didn't want to scare her away. "Just let me love you." He kissed her then, thoroughly, with lots of tongue, while he stroked her full, glorious breasts. Instinctively he'd known she'd feel like this, her skin pulsing and warm beneath his fingers as she arched into his caress.

Her response threatened to end his control and turn him into a rutting beast concerned only with his own satisfaction. He reined in the impulse to abandon the seduction and take her in one satisfying thrust. Lifting his mouth from hers, he began moving down, taking each nipple in his mouth, coaxing her to reward him with soft cries of delight.

She was a banquet, and he was the honored guest. His heart rate jumped as he kissed his way down the valley between her ribs, paid homage to her navel and settled at last between her thighs. Her intoxicating scent rose to meet him as her breath grew ragged.

"Wyatt..."

"I'm here." He lowered his head. "Right...here." He touched down, and she cried out in complete abandon. And that was what he was after, total surrender. He used his tongue to pleasure her and wrenched another cry from her lips. And another, and another, until she filled the morning air with her cries and came in a rush of sweet moisture, her body taut and quivering beneath him.

He'd achieved his initial goal of giving her a climax, but those dreamlike pictures in his mind wouldn't materialize unless they achieved a more basic connection, soul to soul. Rising above her, he sought her pulsing center and drove home.

11

Trembling from her orgasm, Olivia had no breath to ask for what she wanted. She'd come in a shower of pleasure, but an ache remained, one that could only be filled if he would just…yes. He was there. One swift movement of his hips and he was buried deep, joined with her in the way she'd longed for. She hugged him close and wrapped her legs around his, drawing him in tight.

"Easy." His breath was warm against her ear. "Don't hold me too tight or I can't move."

She gulped for air. "I don't want you to move. I want you right there."

He rocked forward. "There?"

"Yes." She lifted her hips, pressing her sensitive trigger spot against his body, pressing, squirming, until… the explosion came again, making her buck in his arms and gasp out his name.

"Ah, Olivia." His soft chuckle tickled the inside of her ear. "My amazing Olivia. Loosen your hold and we can do that again."

Lost in the wonder of her shuddering response, she heard him as if from a distance, but she relaxed her grip, allowing him to move. And move he did, easing away and sliding home in slow, steady strokes.

She moved with him, surrendering to his rhythm, loving the sweet feel of his cock caressing her so intimately. Lovely. Not mind-bending like before, but if this was good for him, then she'd— *Oh*...he shifted, came in from a slightly different angle.

She moaned as he made contact with a spot deeper, more elusive. He sought out that spot again, and yet again. A coil of tension wound within her.

"Tell me." His voice was a low growl. "Is that good?"

She began to pant. "Yes."

"How good?" He moved faster.

"Very...very...oh...Wyatt..."

"This time will be for both of us." His breathing roughened. "Come for me, Olivia. I can't hold off much longer."

She rose to meet him, glorying in the power of each stroke. "Don't wait," she murmured. "Take what you need. Take it!"

With a bellow of satisfaction he pushed deep, and that was all she needed to be hurled over the edge with him. Her spasms blended with his as they clung to each other in the whirlwind they'd created...together.

Gradually his tense muscles relaxed as he settled against her. She welcomed the feel of his warm chest covering her, although he kept the pressure light, not giving her his full weight. She wasn't surprised that he'd be considerate when he was in bed with a woman. He was that kind of guy.

Stroking his back, she listened to his breathing as it evened out and her thoughts returned to her experience on the rock. Standing there with him had felt so...so *right*. If the rock was supposed to give a person mental clarity, then the message she received had been crystal clear. Wyatt was good for her.

She wasn't about to base her whole future on a feeling she'd experienced standing on a piece of quartz and granite, but for that one moment, she'd been convinced Wyatt was the one. Probably just a hormonal reaction.

But something she did know for sure—he was incredible in the sack. She hoped they'd find time for more of this particular activity. Once Jack and the rest of the guys came home, though, that might be tricky.

Outside the truck a bird gave a little concert, trilling and warbling like crazy. "I feel like that bird," she murmured.

"No, you don't." He caressed her bare shoulder. "A bird has feathers."

"I meant I feel like that *inside*."

"That's not true, either. I've been inside, and you're smooth, and warm and very wet, but no feathers."

"You're ridiculous." She pinched his butt.

"Ow."

"I'm trying to tell you I feel happy."

"Good." He nuzzled the side of her neck. "Me too."

"But we probably should head back. I don't want anyone to get worried and come looking for us."

"Good point." Wyatt propped himself up on one elbow and gazed down at her.

She smiled. "But I wouldn't mind doing this again sometime."

"Excellent." He dropped a quick kiss on her mouth. "I'll get dressed outside and leave the camper to you."

His gray eyes glowed with warmth. "See you in a few minutes." Easing away from her, he left the truck.

She took a deep breath. Wow. What a great guy. She sure hoped things worked out with Jack, because she wouldn't mind having Wyatt make that move to Jackson Hole.

On the way back to the ranch Olivia got a little more background on Wyatt's life when he was a kid growing up in San Francisco. He spent way more time describing his friends from high school and college than he did talking about his family. She could understand. Between having a mother like Diana and dealing with her recent divorce from his father, Wyatt would probably like to avoid discussing his family.

When they walked back into the ranch house they met Sarah coming from the wing where her bedroom was located.

"You're just in time for lunch!" She beamed at them as if they were cherished guests. "That hat looks terrific on you, Wyatt."

"I appreciate the loan, but I should give it back to you—"

"Not yet. Keep it until you get one of your own. Anyway, to catch you up on the doings, Pam's gone back to the B and B, but the girls all decided to stick around here for the rest of the day because we don't see as much of each other as we used to now that everyone has her own place. Come on back and have some lunch."

Olivia felt a pang of uneasiness. "You're sweet to invite us, Sarah, but it seems like this is family time."

"Don't be silly. You're like family. Come on down to the dining room with me."

"Olivia's right," Wyatt said. "You deserve some privacy with your daughters-in-law and your grandkids. Besides, we both have things to do and we might as well get them accomplished. I need to go back over to the Bunk and Grub to pick up my stuff, and on the way I can pull Olivia's Jeep out of the ditch."

"Good plan." Olivia appreciated him coming up with a reason to leave.

"Well, I suppose you will have to do those things eventually, so you might as well get them out of the way now, before the men come back."

"Exactly," Wyatt said.

"But I'm inviting you for dinner tonight, Olivia. We'll have a big celebration for the guys coming home from their successful trip. You can either drive yourself or have Wyatt bring you, whatever makes sense. But I've so enjoyed having you here. You fit right in, like you're one of my girls."

For one embarrassing moment Olivia thought she might burst into tears. She'd missed the mothering she'd received from the women at A Cut Above more than she'd realized. She cleared the unexpected emotion from her throat. "Thank you," she said. "I'd like that."

"Good. It's settled, then. What did you think of the sacred site, by the way?"

Olivia's cheeks grew warm. "Fascinating," she said. "Absolutely fascinating."

Sarah gazed at them with a knowing smile. "I thought you'd like it out there."

"It was great." Wyatt's tone was nonchalant, as if all they'd done was take a drive to see the sights. "Thanks for giving us directions."

"You're welcome. Well, I'm sure Mary Lou wonders where I am, so I'd better get back to the kitchen. See you both later. Make sure you get here before dark. That road desperately needs grading after the rain, but you'll find it easier if you can see the ruts."

"Will do," Wyatt said.

Once Sarah was gone, Olivia turned to him. "Nicely handled."

He grinned at her. "You, on the other hand, turned the color of a stop sign."

She groaned. "I know. I'm sorry."

"Don't worry about it. I think Sarah knows something is going on between us. After all, she's raised three boys, so it's not like she doesn't understand. If she disapproved, we'd know it right away."

"I guess so." She glanced at him. "That hat really does look good on you."

"Maybe so, but I doubt I'll be wearing it again. A Stetson doesn't go with hiking shorts and a T-shirt, which is what I'll have on once I've picked up my clothes from the Bunk and Grub."

"I'm guessing you don't want Jack to come home and find you wearing his old clothes."

"Good guess. Or his hat."

"Then let's get on with that program. I'll run upstairs and grab my totes." As she hurried up the stairs, she couldn't help feeling a little sad that she wouldn't be sleeping here tonight. But she had a perfectly fine house that she liked, even if it didn't have the ambiance of the ranch house.

She hadn't realized until staying overnight that part of that ambiance was the scent of varnished logs permeated with wood smoke, overlaid with the aroma of leather and lemon oil furniture polish. The house not only looked like it belonged on a ranch, it smelled as if it did.

She quickly gathered her bags and made sure she hadn't left anything in the bathroom. Maybe Sarah would decide to have another night of beauty at the end of the summer, after the teenagers had left. Olivia hoped so. She'd like to be invited back.

But as she reached the top of the stairs and gazed down at the man waiting for her, she realized that he'd been a big part of the reason she'd loved staying here. She couldn't imagine this place without Wyatt, and yet his continued presence on the ranch wasn't assured. She hoped he wouldn't turn into a bone of contention between Sarah, who wanted him here, and Jack, who hadn't acted as if he did.

Wyatt was right to insist on changing into his own clothes before Jack came home. Sarah might not think anything of it, but if Jack already considered Wyatt an interloper, seeing him in his clothes would make everything worse. Wyatt did look great in them, though. Just looking at him made her hot.

He watched her come down the stairs, a gleam in his eyes that suggested he was having similar thoughts. "Ready?"

She laughed softly. "For what?"

"You're a bad girl, Olivia."

"Don't pretend you're not thinking the same thing, because I can see it in your face."

"Who, me? All I'm thinking about is getting your Jeep out of a ditch."

"Then the prospect of doing that must really turn you on, cowboy."

"I'm not a—"

"Can you ride a horse?"

"Yes."

"Do you respect women?"

His gray eyes twinkled. "Yes."

"Are you kind to old people, kids and animals?"

"Yes." He began to laugh.

"I've watched hundreds of cowboy movies with my dad, and you just passed the test. Plus you look great in those clothes, so I now pronounce you a cowboy."

"If you say so. Now let's go see about your Jeep."

"Oh, that's the other thing. You rescue damsels in distress. Can't forget that."

"Nope." He held the door for her. "I'm not likely to forget it, either. That was the first time I got my hands on you. Here. Let me carry those for you." He took her totes just as music started coming from one of them.

"Let me keep that one. My dad's calling."

"I should have known when I heard the theme from *The Good, the Bad and the Ugly*."

"Oh, yeah. He loves those old Clint Eastwood spaghetti Westerns. Excuse me a minute." Pausing in the gravel driveway, she answered her phone.

"Hey, Livy. Thought you might be home by now."

"Not quite, Dad." She usually spent a couple of hours with him on Sunday playing chess, but she'd warned him she wasn't sure how this Sunday would turn out. Boy, had that been on the money. "Do you need anything?"

"Just wondered if we'd get in that chess game."

"Um, let me give you a call when I get home. I've been invited to come back here for dinner, so I'm not sure how much extra time I'll have."

"Oh, that's okay, Livy. We can skip it."

"Maybe we can schedule it for tomorrow instead."

"If you have time, but don't worry if it doesn't work out." He sounded cheerful, as he always did. She'd never seen her father in a bad mood.

"I'll call you when I get home, Dad. Bye for now. Love you."

"Love you, too, sweetheart."

She disconnected the phone and glanced up to discover Wyatt watching her, and the gleam of desire in his eyes had been replaced by something more poignant. He seemed almost...wistful. "My dad and I usually play chess on Sundays for a few hours," she said. "He just wondered if the game was on or off."

Wyatt perked up. "So you play chess?"

"I do. You?"

"I've been known to. Maybe we should play sometime."

She smiled, recognizing immediately that he was into it. "I warn you, I've been taught to play by a guy who tests out at the genius level on a standard IQ test. But if you're ready to be beat, I'll happily take you on."

"Okay. And just so you know, I can lose to a woman without whimpering."

"Good to hear, because I hate that. Whimpering puts a real damper on my sex drive. Maybe we could take a chess set when we go on that camping trip."

"I'll plan on it."

"Great." But her mind was no longer on chess. From

the moment her dad had called she'd been mulling over a somewhat radical idea. She liked Wyatt. Really liked him. What if he turned out to be like the others she'd thought were nice until they made fun of her dad?

The closer she and Wyatt became, the more she'd worry about that. But not if she took action now. True, she'd risk ending something that had been great so far, but if she didn't take this step she'd risk future disillusionment and heartache. It was a no-brainer.

But she'd have to sound übercasual about it. "After we get my Jeep out, how would you like to follow me home and see my house?"

"Great."

"I probably should stop by my dad's, too, and see if he's low on groceries. I usually check that out when I'm there on Sundays. You can come along, if you want."

"Uh, okay."

She noted he sounded less enthusiastic about that part. "No big deal." She laughed. "It's not like I'm officially taking you to meet him or anything. It's just that I'd like to spend time with you this afternoon, but I should probably at least poke my head in and check out his food situation. You could always wait for me at my house, I guess."

"No, no, I'll go with you." He was making a valiant attempt to cover his reluctance.

She gave him points for that. Her suggestion obviously had taken him by surprise, but he was rolling with it. The more she thought about this plan, the better she liked it.

Her dad was…different, and people couldn't seem to resist commenting on his eccentricities. She could tolerate it when the comments came from casual acquaintances, but not from a guy she had feelings for. Much as she was resistant to admit it, she was beginning to have feelings for Wyatt.

She thought about warning him that most likely the house would be a mess and her dad would be roaming around in his "lab coat," which was really a ratty white bathrobe he loved to wear. If they were lucky he wouldn't offer them something to eat. His food inventions usually combined ingredients never meant to coexist.

But she decided against issuing any warnings or making any defensive statements. The less she said about her father at this point, the more she'd discover what kind of guy Wyatt really was.

12

WYATT CARRIED A TOW CHAIN in his truck and the road had dried enough that hauling Olivia's Jeep out of the ditch didn't take long at all. She seemed impressed with his efficiency and he didn't mind winning more points, but it wasn't a particularly heroic feat.

Meeting her dad would be a much bigger test of his worthiness. Yeah, he was a little apprehensive about that. If it had been up to him he would have put the moment off a while longer. Then again, maybe it was a good thing to get out of the way.

Deciding to pick up his clothes from the Bunk and Grub on the way back to the ranch, he followed Olivia to her house, a neat little two-story Victorian on a side street a block away from Shoshone's central business district. On a Sunday afternoon the streets were deserted.

He parked behind her in the driveway next to the house. The place was old enough to have a detached garage, but someone had kept the property in tip-top shape. The house was painted a sunny yellow with white trim. Two hanging baskets of petunias brightened the front porch along with a couple of white wicker rockers.

Wyatt liked the whole rocker-on-the-porch concept, although he still hadn't taken advantage of the ones at the ranch. He couldn't complain, though. He'd much rather have spent the morning having hot sex with Olivia than lounging on the porch at the Last Chance.

She climbed down from her Jeep and then pulled her totes out. "We can walk to my dad's from here," she said. "I called him from the road and I'm afraid he insisted on making us lunch. I tried to talk him out of it, but in the end it was easier just to agree."

"That's fine." He had a hunch that an eccentric genius might come up with some oddball combinations, but at least the guy sounded hospitable. Good thing Wyatt had a cast-iron stomach.

"I appreciate you being flexible. I just need to put my bags inside. Come on in and see the place."

"Thanks." He followed her over to the small porch, curious to see what her house would look like.

"I'm still getting settled." She opened the screen door and shoved the key in the lock. "I didn't bring much with me from Pittsburgh. What I had wasn't really worth moving, the kind of secondhand stuff you buy when you're starting out."

"Right." He'd have to take her word for it. When he'd moved into his first apartment, his mother had insisted he take all the rec room furniture, which she pronounced "ruined" after the one and only party he'd had for friends after graduating from college. One coffee table had a slight scratch. Technically it was secondhand, but not the way Olivia meant it.

He followed her through the front door with its leaded-glass insert and found himself in a room full of rainbows. Sunlight streamed through the living room windows and the faceted crystals she had hanging in them.

"Beautiful," he murmured.

"Cheap decorating. It kind of makes up for the lack of furniture."

"Yeah, but what you have is great." An overstuffed sofa covered in denim with a couple of colorful throw pillows was the only piece in the room other than a cabinet holding a small flat-screen TV. It was what Wyatt thought of as a make-out couch—long, wide and cushy.

Too bad he and Olivia had other things to do. He had no trouble imagining how he could draw her down on those plump cushions and coax her out of her clothes. He still had a condom burning a hole in his pocket.

"We should go," she said gently. "I told my dad we were on our way."

He snapped out of his erotic daze.

Olivia had put down her bags and was gazing at him with amusement.

"Sorry. But it's a great sofa."

"I thought so when I bought it."

He decided there was no point in being subtle. "I was thinking about how much fun we could have on it."

"I could tell."

He noticed that her eyes were about the same color as the sofa. She'd look awesome lying naked on it. "I want to kiss you so much right now, but if I do it would lead to the sofa. So let's head outside before my self-control disintegrates and I grab you."

She smiled. "Okay."

He felt very noble as he followed her out the door. "Going to lock it?"

"Nope. That's another thing I love about this place. I can run down to my dad's for a while and not worry about locking up. When I'm going to be gone longer than that, I usually do, just so the wind won't blow the door open and let in the birds and the squirrels. But I don't worry about thieves."

Wyatt took her hand as they started down the tree-shaded sidewalk. "I'd like living like that. It's not an option in my apartment building in San Francisco."

"I can't picture you in the city."

"I'm not there much. I always figured it was as good a home base as any for Adventure Trekking, since most of my clients come through my website. I've never thought it mattered where I lived, but then again, I never look forward to going home either."

"It's good to have a place that welcomes you when you walk through the door."

"You've certainly accomplished that."

She laughed. "I didn't realize how seductive that sofa was until you stepped inside my living room. Suddenly all I could think about was rolling around on it with you."

"I'm glad I wasn't the only one with a one-track mind." He squeezed her hand. "But if I'm about to meet your father, I need to get that image out of my head. In my experience, dads have a sixth sense for identifying guys with designs on their daughters."

"Not mine. He assumes that if I allowed you into my life, then you're A-okay."

"So he trusts you." Wyatt now understood why a disparaging remark about her father would cause Olivia to cut that person off at the knees. Given the unwavering confidence her dad had placed in her, she wasn't about to let him be hurt by an unkind comment.

"He does trust me," she said. "And I don't take that lightly."

"I'm sure." He loved how the sunlight brought out little flecks of gold in her blue eyes. "I'm having another one of those I-want-to-kiss-you moments."

She reached up and pressed her finger gently against his mouth. "Later," she murmured as she came to a halt on the sidewalk. "We're here."

The brick bungalow wasn't as cheerful-looking as Olivia's house, but the front yard was neat and the porch had a swing. The front door was painted dark purple.

"Interesting door," Wyatt said cautiously as they approached the house.

"Dad's choice. He thinks it's a good color for wizardry."

"Ah." Wyatt hoped to hell he was up for this. "So do you knock on the door, or say magic words, or what?"

"Nothing. He knows we're here and he'll open the door."

"He was watching at the window?"

"Nope. We just tripped a laser beam about six inches above the top porch step. It sounds a chime inside the house."

The purple door opened and Wyatt decided that Olivia's father was indeed a wizard, or at least a good impersonation of one. Tall and thin, he wore a long white robe and black sandals. His white hair puffed out from his head like dandelion seeds about to take flight. Wire-rimmed glasses perched on his long nose, which brought Wyatt's attention to piercing blue eyes. All the man needed was a staff topped with a dragon's head and he could audition for a *Lord of the Rings* production.

"Hi, Dad." Olivia stepped forward and kissed his cheek. "This is Wyatt Locke, the guy who pulled me out of a ditch this morning. Wyatt, I'd like you to meet my father, Grover Sedgewick."

Wyatt stuck out his hand. "It's a pleasure, Mr. Sedgewick. Or is it Professor Sedgewick?"

"Nope, nope." His grip was firm. "Dropped out of college. Never could get the hang of academia. And call me Grover, son. It sounds friendlier. Come on in. Lunch is ready."

Wyatt followed Olivia into a house that smelled sharp and tangy, as if it had been soaked in vinegar. The living room was chaotic, with papers and books scattered on the floor and covering the furniture. Stirring classical music played in the background, the kind with lots of drums and French horns.

Among the books and papers Wyatt caught glimpses of gadgets—creations involving wires and batteries and strangely shaped pieces of metal. The only orderly surface he could find was the wall opposite the front door.

There, marching in neat rows in an area at least four by eight feet, were framed pictures of Olivia from babyhood to womanhood. A few looked quite recent. Then the display moved on to certificates from elementary school through high school for things like spelling bees, making the honor roll and good citizenship. Wyatt had never seen more touching evidence of parental pride than this.

"That's my girl." Grover swept a hand toward the wall, just in case Wyatt might have missed it. "She's a corker."

"Yes, sir, she is." Wyatt couldn't help smiling. *Corker* was an old-fashioned word, but it fit Olivia.

Instead of being embarrassed because her father insisted on splashing her early history all over his living room wall, she simply put her arm around him and gave him a hug. "Thanks, Dad." She gazed at him with fondness. "You're a corker, too."

As she stood serenely in this disaster of a house with a father who greeted a guest in his bathrobe, Wyatt looked at her with new respect and admiration. He'd always known this was a woman he could like, and certainly a woman he could lust after. At that moment, he realized she was also a woman he could love.

THEY ATE IN THE DINING ROOM, where Olivia's father had cleared off enough of the papers to make room for three plates. Olivia watched Wyatt swallow a hot dog and peanut butter concoction without a grimace or complaint. He didn't flinch when her father brought out his "bug juice" as a complement to the meal, even though it was a ghastly shade of blue.

Lunch was a slightly larger test than she'd planned on, but she was impressed with the way Wyatt soldiered cheerfully through the meal. After having suffered through her dad's cooking all her life, she knew the food could have been worse. She was relieved that today's lunch was at least recognizable.

Conversation revolved around Wyatt's job and his reason for coming to the area. Grover seemed pleased that Wyatt was Jack Chance's half brother and might end up moving to Shoshone. Because her dad wasn't privy to community gossip, he didn't know that Wyatt and Jack's mother was persona non grata in town. Wyatt didn't bring that up, which kept the tone positive, the way her father preferred it.

As the meal wound to a close, her dad glanced over at Wyatt. "You strike me as a chess-playing man."

Wyatt sent Olivia a questioning look.

She held up both hands. "I didn't mention it. If my dad likes somebody, he usually asks if they play chess."

Wyatt seemed pleased with that. "As a matter of fact, Grover, I play a little."

"Care for a game?"

Olivia crossed her fingers. If her father suggested a chess game, that meant he wanted to get to know Wyatt better. Grover believed in learning about people by observing them during a chess match.

Once again Wyatt glanced at Olivia. "Okay with you?"

She shrugged, as if it didn't matter one way or the other. "Sure."

"All right, then, Grover. Let's set up the board."

Olivia relaxed. She hadn't realized until that moment how tense she'd felt as she'd watched the two men interact. But it would be okay. Anyone who could eat Grover's cooking with as much grace as Wyatt had could also handle being annihilated in a chess game.

To her surprise and delight, Wyatt played a decent first game. Her father still beat him handily, but then her father beat everyone handily. A couple of times in the twenty years she'd been playing him, she'd come really close to winning a game. Anyone who could give her father even a slight challenge was aces in his book.

In the second game Wyatt actually managed to make her father pause and stroke his chin, a sign that he didn't immediately know his next move. Olivia gazed at Wyatt with new respect. Not many accomplished that.

"Did I stump you, Grover?" Wyatt took another sip of his blue drink.

"Momentarily." Her dad studied the board. "Aha." Then he proceeded to take command of the game once again.

As Wyatt went down in flames for the second time, taking his defeat without excuses and complimenting her dad on his playing, Olivia longed to wrap her arms around this amazing guy and hold on tight. She thought of the way he'd looked at her sofa, and glanced at the time on her phone. The afternoon was getting away from them.

"I hate to break this up." She thought the lie was forgivable under the circumstances. "But Wyatt and I need to get moving if we're going to finish our other little chores before we head back to the ranch for dinner."

Wyatt pushed back his chair. "Guess so." He held out his hand to Grover. "You're a tough competitor and I'm looking forward to a rematch."

"Any time." Grover stood. "Any friend of Olivia's is a friend of mine."

"She mentioned that, and I feel lucky that she considers me a friend."

Grover nodded, his white hair bobbing. "You are

lucky. I need to warn you that she's picky, though. She's given three men the boot already, back when we lived in Pittsburgh."

"Because they were jerks," Olivia said. She hadn't told her father the exact reason she'd broken up with all three of those guys, and she didn't intend to.

"I think there was a little more to it than that," her father said with a smile. "But I guess it helps if you don't act like a jerk."

"I'll do my best not to, sir."

"I hope so. I'd like to keep you on as a chess partner. Now run along, both of you. I know you have things to do. Thanks for spending some time with an old man."

"You're not old, Dad." Olivia gave him a hug and a kiss on the cheek. "You're timeless. I'll call you to-morrow."

"I'd like that."

Once they were out the door, Olivia laced her fingers through Wyatt's. "Thank you. You were terrific."

Terrific didn't even cover it. He'd passed this test with flying colors, but she had to be careful not to overdo her compliments or he might suspect he'd been set up.

"You say that like I was making some sort of sacrifice. I had a blast."

"Well, I could see you were engaged in the chess game, and he is an outstanding player, but I can't believe you were okay with the food."

Wyatt laughed. "It was like being back at Scout camp when we used to dream up every gross combination we could think of. I'm pretty sure we had hot dogs and peanut butter once. It tasted very familiar."

"You really didn't mind it?"

"Hell, no! Even the bug juice made me nostalgic for those days at camp. Considering my home life, I *loved* camp. One of the counselors taught us how to play chess. I was in my element just now."

She hadn't expected that kind of response in a million years. "Then maybe I shouldn't have dragged you away."

"Oh, yeah, you should."

"But if you were having so much fun, you probably wanted to stay and wallow in nostalgia some more."

"I might have, if I hadn't known there was a certain cushy sofa waiting for us over at your house."

Now she felt better. "You think that's why I suggested we had to leave? So we could roll around naked on that sofa?"

"I hope so, because if that's not what you have in mind, then I'm going back for another game of chess with your dad."

She tightened her grip on his fingers. "My dad's had his time with you. Now it's my turn."

13

OLIVIA'S HEART RATE HAD skyrocketed by the time she and Wyatt reached her front door. "We'll have to lower the blinds," she said.

"I'll leave that to you." His voice was low and urgent. "I'm feeling so desperate I might pull the damned blind right out of the window casing, and then what would we do?"

"Go back to my bedroom." Nothing was going to stop her from having her way with him.

"Maybe we should do that in the first place. Just because I have an image of you naked on that sofa, doesn't mean—"

"Yes, it does. Anybody can do it on a bed." She drew him through the door. "Let's make some memories on the sofa."

"Yeah, let's." Shoving the door closed with his booted foot, he pulled her into his arms and kissed her feverishly as he began divesting her of her clothes. He behaved as if he couldn't get enough of her.

"The blinds…" she gasped between kisses. "We have to…"

"I know. In a minute. I just need to—" Pulling her T-shirt over her head, he unhooked her bra.

"You're crazy," she murmured, but she was just as busy unsnapping his shirt and running both hands up his lightly furred chest. "I love how you feel."

"I love how you feel, more." Cupping her breasts, he leaned down and sucked an aching nipple into his mouth.

She forgot all about the blinds. Nothing mattered but his hands, his mouth, his tongue. They wriggled out of their clothes, laughing as her zipper stuck and his boots refused to come off his feet. Her zipper finally gave way but his boots weren't so cooperative.

"I can do this with my boots on, damn it. And my jeans." He stripped hers away. "At least one of us is naked." His voice was thick with need. "The most critical one."

"I don't know about that." She was panting by the time she flopped back on the sofa. "I think you should be—"

"—kissing you all over." Kneeling beside the sofa, his shirt and his jeans unbuttoned and unzipped but still on, he proceeded to do exactly that. "You've covered with rainbows."

"That's because the blinds...are still up."

"I can't bring myself to care." He circled her nipple with his tongue.

Neither could she. She abandoned herself to the sensuous pleasure of lying naked on her sofa while Wyatt hovered over her, bestowing erotic kisses.

"There's a rainbow here." He licked the underside of

her breast. "And another one here." He touched down just beneath her navel. "Oh, and one more here."

She didn't know whether a rainbow rested at the sensitive spot where he put his mouth last, but she wasn't going to question his word. She'd experienced his expertise at this endeavor before, and she was willing to believe a rainbow had guided him there.

She was willing to believe anything he told her when he was doing…oh, yes…*that.*

"I love how you taste," he murmured, his breath hot against her moist skin. He slid both hands under her. "And how you make that little noise in the back of your throat when I do this." He settled in and began to get serious.

She had no idea what little noise he meant, because her brain had turned to mush. She probably made that noise, along with several others, as he nibbled and licked and generally drove her insane. She vaguely remembered begging him to make her come, and he did… gloriously.

As she vibrated from the intensity of it, she heard boots hit the floor and the clank of a belt buckle followed. A foil package was ripped open and then he was there, managing the gymnastics necessary to make love to her on a sofa that was almost, but not quite, long enough.

Or wide enough. She put one foot on the floor and so did he. They maneuvered and shifted, their laughter breathless, their excitement building along with their frustration.

"I know what," he said at last. "Let me sit on the sofa and you——"

"Brilliant." Which was how she ended up straddling him in the center of the middle cushion, her hands braced on his shoulders as she rode him to glory, both his and hers.

Gasping for breath, they touched foreheads.

"I love this sofa," he said. "Don't ever get rid of it."

"I won't." She gulped for air. "It's a part of history now."

"Yeah." He slid his hands from her hips to her waist. "Our first ride together."

She probably should be worried that they were talking about furniture as a history of their relationship, as if it was destined to last a very long time. But he'd been so great with her dad, and in her warm, postorgasmic glow, she couldn't be bothered to worry about anything.

True, she hadn't known him very long, and she'd promised herself that she'd take her time about singling out another guy. But Wyatt had shown himself to be a hero in so many ways already. What could possibly go wrong?

ALTHOUGH WYATT WASN'T crazy about the idea of driving back to the ranch separately, he couldn't argue with the logic of it. Olivia wanted time to shower and change clothes, and he needed to go back to the Bunk and Grub and get his things. He'd called the ranch and the travelers weren't expected for at least another hour, so he had time to shower and change, too.

After dinner Olivia would go home. Not knowing how tonight would turn out, Wyatt thought it was probably best if they each had their own transportation. He expected to spend the night at the ranch, but if things went south with Jack, Wyatt could always ask if Olivia would take him in temporarily.

With a mental promise to return at some point in time, he left the yellow house with the white trim, the rainbows, and the most excellent blue denim sofa, not to mention the amazing woman he'd made love to there. He was comfortable with the term *made love* when it came to Olivia. Their connection deepened with every moment they spent together.

He would not, however, pursue her. He would love her with everything he had to offer and hope that she would pursue him. It wasn't the way he normally handled events in his life, but he was willing to adapt to the situation.

When he arrived at the Bunk and Grub, he sought out Pam in the little office she'd created right next to the living room.

She turned in her wooden swivel chair with a smile of greeting. Her blond bob shone in the afternoon light coming through a window. "I knew you'd show up sometime, but I wasn't sure when. I have your duffel bag over in the corner, ready to go. How has your day been?"

"Incredible." As he said it, he realized he'd put a hell of a lot of emotion into that one word. Probably too much if he wanted to keep things under wraps.

"It's Olivia." Pam wasn't asking. It probably only took one look at his smiling face to know, especially after seeing them gravitating toward each other last night.

"Yeah." He sighed. "It's Olivia."

"She's great. I hope you two continue to get along. Listen, do you have a minute to sit and talk?"

"Sure." He levered himself into a wingback chair in the corner of Pam's tiny office. "But first off, I want to pay you for the nights I booked here. It's not right to reserve a room and then cancel at the last minute."

Pam gazed at him. "I don't know how much you know about me."

"A little. You own this place, and you're Nick's aunt, and from what you said last night, there's some connection to Emmett Sterling, the ranch foreman."

Pam chuckled. "Oh, there is. I've had a serious crush on that guy for years, which isn't surprising. He looks like Tom Selleck and is a real sweetheart and a good dad to Emily. But he's not what you'd call wealthy, and I...am."

Wyatt nodded. "My dad's around that age, and I don't know if he could accept being with a woman who was richer than he is."

"I intend to keep working on Emmett, but the real point I wanted to make is that I don't need the money from that reservation. But if you're determined to pay it, I'll accept on one condition."

"What's that?"

"As you can imagine, Sarah and I had a couple of conversations about you."

Warmth crept up the back of Wyatt's neck. "I'm sure she's worried about whether my presence will cause trouble. That's one reason I wanted to stay with you, but Sarah wouldn't hear of it."

"Of course she wouldn't. Jack may be part owner of the ranch but Sarah still wields most of the power over there. You came with good intentions, and she wants you to feel welcome. She doesn't think anyone should tiptoe around Jack on this issue."

Wyatt nodded. "Okay. I respect that."

"But she realizes that having Jack come home to find you in his old clothes might start things off on the wrong foot."

"Exactly. That's one of the main reasons I'm picking up my things, so I can go back to the ranch and change into my own stuff."

"Shorts and T-shirts, right?"

"That's what I live in."

"It's anyone's guess what the best strategy is when it comes to Jack, but Sarah and I think it might be better if you looked less like a California dude and more like a cowboy. Besides, you can't ride a horse in shorts, and if you want to bond with Jack you'll do it best on horseback. That's where he feels most at home."

"Guess I'll go shopping first thing in the morning, then. I'd thought about doing that, anyway." Not so much for Jack, but for Olivia, who seemed to like his cowboy look.

"Or…" Pam left her desk and opened a small coat closet. "You can accept these things I picked up today in Jackson." She took a shopping bag out and brought it over to where Wyatt sat, openmouthed. "Once Sarah knew you fit into Jack's old clothes, she was able to give me the size. I've taken all the tags off because I want you to consider them a gift. I wasn't lucky enough to have kids of my own, so I spoil those Chance boys rotten and I'd be tickled to do the same with you."

Wyatt looked from the bag to Pam. She'd driven

to Jackson and spent her valuable time and money on him, someone she barely knew. He was overwhelmed by her thoughtfulness and generosity. "I don't know what to say."

"Say, 'thank you, Pam,' and then hop in your truck and head out to the ranch so you can change clothes before Jack and the other guys get home."

"Thank you, Pam." He stood and gave her a hug. In the past twenty-four hours Sarah and Pam had acted more like mothers to him than his own ever had.

"If you don't like anything I can take it back, even without the tags. They know me there."

He grinned. "I'm sure they do, but I'm not giving anything back. I'll proudly wear every stitch until it falls off me."

"One other thing. I didn't buy boots, but I don't think wearing Jack's will be a big issue. And I didn't get you a hat, either. That's something you should probably pick out for yourself. A cowboy's hat is kind of like his signature."

"Got it. Thanks, Pam. You're the best." With a heart full of gratitude he picked up the bag, grabbed his duffel from the corner, and left the Bunk and Grub.

Olivia had told him he had support in his quest to make friends with his half brother and his extended family. Apparently that was true. Now all he needed was for Jack to arrive home feeling mellow from the success of his trip and in the mood to give friendship one last chance. If Jack would just meet him halfway, Wyatt was willing to do the rest.

LESS THAN AN HOUR LATER, Wyatt finally had his first opportunity to sit on the ranch's front porch in one of the wooden rockers. After taking a quick shower and putting on one of his new pairs of jeans and a pale green yoked shirt, he'd come downstairs and discovered everyone had gathered on the porch with wine, beer and snacks to await the arrival of what Sarah had dubbed "our returning heroes."

Apparently the final tally of horses sold and stud fees collected was very good financial news for the Last Chance. Wyatt got the impression that the family sometimes struggled with being land-rich and cash-poor, but that wouldn't be the case this summer. He was happy for them.

Peter Beckett, a tall, distinguished guy in his mid-sixties, had come for the welcoming party. Sarah introduced Peter, and Wyatt liked his easy smile and firm handshake. Wyatt wasn't sure if he was supposed to congratulate them on their engagement or not.

"Sarah tells me the cat's out of the bag," Peter said, ending Wyatt's uncertainty. "Looks like I'll be joining the family soon."

"I heard that," Wyatt said. "I haven't been here long, but I can already say that anyone who's allowed to hook up with the Chance family is one lucky SOB."

"I totally agree."

"Thanks, Wyatt." Sarah leaned over and gave him a kiss on the cheek. "You look great."

"Pam's a persuasive woman." He smiled at her. "Like I said, hooking up with the Chance family comes with all sorts of benefits."

She beamed with happiness and linked her arm through Peter's. "I'm glad you think so. Now, go get yourself a cold beer and snag yourself a seat. They should be here soon."

"You bet." Feeling as if this might go well after all, he pulled a beer from a much larger cooler stocked with far more bottles than Mary Lou had provided the night before. This was shaping up to be quite a party.

Josie called him over to an empty rocker next to her. He couldn't help thinking that the chair had been saved for him because Josie wanted Jack to see immediately that she'd accepted Wyatt. Rodney padded over and plopped down at his feet. Wyatt grinned and leaned down to scratch behind the dog's floppy ears.

Josie glanced over at Wyatt as she bounced little Archie gently on her knee. "Nice duds, cowboy. Glad to see you accepted Pam's generosity."

"You knew about that?"

She chuckled. "Oh, yeah. Sarah told us what she and Pam had cooked up and we all speculated as to your reaction. You made the right choice. Pam would have been crushed if you'd refused."

"I was touched that she'd do such a thing when she barely knows me."

"You made friends here last night, Wyatt. We all want this to work out for you. Even the dog."

"Thanks, but don't feel you have to step into the breach if it starts going downhill with Jack. As I said before, I don't want to cause a problem, either between you and Jack, or Sarah and Jack."

"Then Jack will just have to behave himself, won't he?"

Wyatt smiled at her. "Guess so." He uncapped his beer and glanced toward the road. From the moment

he'd come down he'd been watching for Olivia's Cherokee and hoping she'd show up before the men did. But
the road was still empty.

He turned back to Josie. "Did you have a good day?"

"We did. Between working at the Spirits and Spurs
and taking care of Archie, I don't get much chance to
hang out with Sarah and my sisters-in-law." She smiled
at him. "But you could have stayed for lunch, you know.
Sarah said you were afraid you'd be intruding."

"Yeah, I did feel that way. And then it turned out I
got to meet Olivia's dad."

"Really." Josie stopped bouncing Archie. "She's very
careful who she takes over there, for obvious reasons.
Does she know that you know why she broke up with
her fiancés?"

"Nope." He gazed down the road.

"Well, I won't say anything. What did you think of
him?"

Wyatt took a sip of his beer. "He's a genius, is what
he is. You don't meet many of those."

"True." Archie began to fuss so Josie went back to
jiggling him on her knee. "You like her a lot, don't you?"

"Yeah, I do."

"I have a good feeling about you two. It's early yet,
but if you didn't run for the hills after meeting Grover,
that's a good sign." She picked up Archie and scooted
out of the rocker. "Time to walk around with my little
guy. He's getting restless."

Wyatt set his beer down next to his rocker and stood.
"Why don't you let me do that? My nephew and I need
to get better acquainted."

"That would be lovely." She handed him over. "But if he gets too fussy bring him back."

"He won't be fussy, will you, Arch?" He adjusted the baby in his arms and Archie looked at him with wide blue eyes. Wyatt felt a tug of recognition. Archie really did look like Rafe's baby pictures. "Come on, kid. Time to see the sights with Uncle Wyatt."

Carrying the little boy, he walked carefully down the steps, mindful of not stumbling with his precious cargo. Archie seemed to enjoy the movement and change of scenery, so Wyatt walked away from the house and down toward a corral next to the barn where a couple of paint horses milled around. Archie might like watching them.

As he drew closer to the corral, the little kid started crowing and bouncing in his arms, obviously excited about the animals. Wyatt was congratulating himself on being a really cool uncle when he heard the rumble of a truck's engine.

He turned to see a cherry-red semi tractor rig pull in, hauling a large horse trailer. Wyatt watched with a feeling of inevitability as air brakes hissed and the semi came to a halt. Jack Chance climbed down from the driver's side.

14

JACK STARED AT WYATT in obvious disbelief. "You've got my kid!"

A couple of other smaller trucks pulled in behind the horse trailer and Josie hurried down the hill, followed by the rest of the family. Even from this distance Wyatt could see the panic in her expression.

"Hello, Jack," Wyatt said. "Nice to see you again, too."

"What are you doing with my kid?"

"Giving Josie a break. Archie was starting to fuss, so I offered to—"

"You come to my house unannounced when I'm not even here. Don't you own a cell phone?"

"I should have called in advance." Guilt stabbed him.

"Damn straight you should have. This is the second time you've shown up without warning, and I don't like being caught off guard. Not only that, but I arrive home to find you toting my son around like you and he are the best of buds. I don't know much of anything about you, Wyatt Locke, except that you're Diana's son, and that's not much of a recommendation."

Josie reached him, puffing slightly from her short jog. "Jack, I told Wyatt he could carry Archie around."

"Well, if it's all the same to you, I'd rather he didn't do that." Jack closed the distance in two strides and pulled Archie out of Wyatt's arms.

"Wyatt is Archie's uncle, Jack."

Jack glanced at her. "Yeah, and that makes Diana Archie's biological grandmother, which is a sickening thought." His gaze swung to Wyatt. "Did you tell her about Archie?"

"No."

"That's a damn good thing because she has no right to this kid. He's a Chance."

"Jack…" Josie put a hand on his arm.

Jack ignored her and continued to glare at Wyatt. "You, on the other hand, are not. So keep your hands off my kid."

"You arrogant SOB." Anger curdled in Wyatt's gut.

"Jack, stop this!" Josie grabbed hold of his arm.

"Stay out of it, Josie."

"Then give me Archie." Her voice was laced with fury.

"Yeah, take him." Keeping his attention on Wyatt, Jack handed her the baby. "Get him out of here."

Wyatt clenched his fists. He wasn't going to throw the first punch, but he was sorely tempted now that Jack wasn't holding Archie. "How dare you taunt me with not being a Chance, like I had a choice in the matter? Like you did? It's all an accident of birth, Jack."

"This is *my* property, and I dare whatever I damn well please."

"Oh, yeah, the mighty Jack Chance. Judging from your arrogant attitude, I'm glad I'm *not* a Chance!"

"If that's the way you feel, why the hell did you come back?"

"God knows. But I'll tell you this. You should get down on your knees every day and thank God that my mother left you here."

"Oh, but she didn't leave *you,* now, did she?" Jack's expression was thunderous. "You didn't have to wake up one morning and find out that your mother was gone and she wasn't coming back! You didn't have to—"

"You didn't have to grow up with a mother who didn't give a damn about you! And a father who was so busy trying to please her that he barely noticed you either!" Wyatt's blood ran hot in his veins. "No, you were surrounded by people who loved you—your dad, your grandparents and later on Sarah, and this…this whole fricking *ranch!* Yeah, let's compare notes and see who had the worst of it, shall we?"

Archie started to wail at the top of his lungs.

"Get off my land." Jack's face was like granite.

"Don't worry. I've lost any desire to be here." Adrenaline pumping through his system, he stormed past Jack and the rest of the family. Sarah called out to him, and he gave her a wave that he hoped would let her know he heard her, but he couldn't respond. Not now.

When he reached the drive, Olivia had just pulled in. She hopped down, took one look at his face and came running over. "Wyatt?"

"I'm leaving, Olivia." He started up the steps. He felt as if someone had his chest in a vice and was jabbing his head with an ice pick. "You should stay, though. It's going to be a good party, and I know how much you like these folks."

"So do you!" She went up the steps with him. "Are you going to let Jack run you off?"

"I don't stay where I'm not wanted, Olivia." He drew a breath that made his lungs burn. Then he opened the front door and held it for her because she seemed determined to follow him. "Jack was here first, and all I'll do is cause tension if I stay." He didn't break stride as he headed upstairs. "I still love the area, so...we'll see."

Olivia kept pace with him. "So you're not going camping with Jack, I take it?"

His bark of laughter sounded loud in the quiet house. "Hardly."

"Will you take me, then?"

"What?" He reached the second floor and walked quickly down to the room he'd been assigned.

"Camping. Let's go."

"That's crazy." He hadn't taken time to unpack, so all he had to do was throw a few things in his duffel and zip it. He took the bag of clothes Pam had given him as well. He wasn't sure what to do about those, but he could decide that later. "We can't just go off camping."

"Why not?"

"Because..." He actually didn't have a good reason. He had some dehydrated food in the truck, plus water he always carried. He glanced at Olivia's outfit, noticing for the first time that she'd worn sneakers with her jeans and shirt, and she was carrying a zip-up sweatshirt.

"I'm not going to stay for the party if you're leaving," she said. "I came to be with you."

"I don't think I'm going to be very good company."

But the idea of heading off into the woods appealed to him. He'd cancelled his reservation at the Bunk and Grub, and he wouldn't want to stay there anyway.

"Let's do it, Wyatt. I don't have to work tomorrow. Let's spend the night together in a tent. You can teach me how to camp."

"You've been the best part of this whole experience, Olivia."

She smiled at him. "Thanks."

"All righty, then. Let's go camping. You can follow me out, and once we're off the ranch we'll figure out our next move."

"Works for me."

But when they descended the steps, they found Sarah waiting for them. Wyatt looked around for the others but Sarah appeared to be alone in the house, at least for now. She looked extremely determined.

Wyatt's gut tightened again as he walked down the stairs toward her. "Sarah, I'm really sorry. I hate that I spoiled your great homecoming celebration."

"You didn't," she said. "My son did, and I'm sure eventually he'll apologize to you for that."

Wyatt stared at her. "You're kidding, right?"

"No. One of the things I've instilled in all my boys is good manners. Jack forgot his just now, but I have every confidence he'll remember them soon."

There was a hint of steel in her words, but she kept her voice so even that it took Wyatt a moment to realize that she was furious. She did not, however, apologize for Jack. The glint in her eyes made it clear he would be expected to do that for himself.

Wyatt had no stomach for watching a battle of wills

between mother and son, not when he was the bone of contention. "It's okay, Sarah," he said gently. "You've been great to me and I appreciate that."

"I'd rather you didn't leave."

"We're going camping," Olivia said. "So I won't be here for dinner, after all. Thank you for asking me, though."

Sarah frowned. "Camping? Just like that? What about food?"

"I always carry emergency rations in my truck. We'll be fine for one night."

"That's ridiculous. Come back to the kitchen with me."

"No, really." Wyatt didn't want to linger. "We should just go. It's better if we—"

"No one's coming up to the house until I give the okay, so don't get nervous. I instructed them all to stay down by the barn until I'd had an opportunity to talk with you. Pete's in charge of making sure that's the way it goes."

"Wow," Olivia said. "You really are in charge around here."

"You bet your sweet bippy. Now come along. I'll give you some real food so you don't have to eat that reconstituted junk." Sarah marched down the hall toward the dining room and kitchen area.

Wyatt glanced over at Olivia and shrugged. Crossing Sarah right now didn't seem like a wise idea. He set down his duffel and bag of clothes, took Olivia's hand and followed Sarah to the kitchen.

Moments later they came back down the hall. Wyatt carried a soft-sided ice chest filled with frozen gel packs and stuffed with homemade spaghetti sauce, eggs, bacon and cheese. Olivia had a bag that contained a box of pasta, a loaf of homemade bread, a box of crackers and a box of red wine.

Wyatt mentally calculated whether he could get everything in his pack. He might need Olivia to carry some of the food in his spare backpack, but he'd make sure her load was light. He wanted to hike in a ways before they made camp. Getting away from civilization had never seemed more necessary than now.

"Thank you, Sarah." Wyatt glanced at Olivia. "Would you be okay with returning the ice chest and anything we don't use?"

"I expect you to return it, Wyatt," Sarah said. "I can understand that you want to go off and lick your wounds, but you need to come back."

Wyatt faced her. "I'm not sure I even want to—"

"Now you listen to me, Wyatt Locke. You started this thing, and I intend to see that you and Jack are on civil terms before you leave the ranch."

"But—"

"Just leave Olivia's Jeep here, take your truck and drive on up the road past the sacred site. The terrain rises some, and I'm sure you'll find good camping up there."

"I don't want to stay on ranch land."

"Oh, for pity's sake. Of course you do. It's getting late, and you need to make camp before it gets dark. You really don't have time to mess around looking for some other spot, Wyatt. Besides, this way you can come back tomorrow and sort this thing out with Jack."

"I don't think Jack wants to sort it out."

Sarah met his gaze and her jaw firmed. "He will."

Wyatt had never met a woman like Sarah Chance. She was one of the most loving people he'd ever known, yet also one of the toughest. He now understood why she hadn't crumbled when her husband died unexpectedly.

He still didn't believe that he and Jack would mend any fences but he wasn't going to convince Sarah of that, at least not now. Might as well go along with her plan for the time being, especially when he couldn't refute her logic. He might have trouble finding a good camping spot before dark if he insisted on leaving Chance land to do it.

"All right," he said. "I'll take your suggestion. Thank you for everything, Sarah."

"You're welcome. See you tomorrow." She stood in the doorway as they walked down the porch steps and over to Wyatt's truck.

He was aware of her watching as they loaded everything and got into the cab. Once he put the truck in gear and started toward the road leading to the sacred site, she came out on the porch and waved to the group of people waiting down by the barn.

In his rearview mirror, Wyatt saw them trooping back up to the house except for one lone figure. Wyatt was pretty sure he recognized Jack standing there, staring after the truck. His gut twisted again. He'd wanted Jack's goodwill more than he'd realized. But despite Sarah's determination, he doubted he'd ever get it.

OLIVIA WASN'T SURE WHETHER to talk to Wyatt or leave him in peace to mull over his situation. They rode with the windows down, which at least kept the drive from being silent. Small birds twittered in the meadows they passed and a hawk circled overhead and added its piercing cry to the lilting music below.

"The hawk is probably planning to eat one of those songbirds," Wyatt said.

"Now there's a cheerful thought."

"I warned you that I might not be very good company."

Olivia sighed. "Then I say let's talk about what happened instead of sitting here in silence."

"Not much to tell."

"How did everything get nasty so fast? It looked to me as if they'd just come home."

"Bad timing, maybe even poor judgment on my part. We were all sitting on the porch and little Archie started to fuss, so I told Josie I'd walk with him a little, give him a change of scenery."

She could imagine what came next. Poor Wyatt. "Let me guess. Jack came home when you were strolling around with Archie."

"I don't know why I didn't think that might happen. I was just enjoying taking the little guy down to see the horses, and somehow it didn't occur to me that Jack might not react well to me doing that. The minute I heard that heavy-duty engine, I knew I was screwed."

She reached over and rubbed his thigh. "I'm sorry." Then she paused. "Are these new? They don't feel like jeans that have been worn a lot."

Wyatt smiled for the first time since she'd met him coming up from the barn. "I think you should feel that material again to make real sure it's different from the jeans Sarah loaned me."

She was encouraged by that remark. Leaning over, she stroked his thigh again. "These are not the jeans you borrowed from Sarah."

"So do you like this feel better than the ones I had on before? Go right ahead and fondle them again if you're not sure. I don't mind."

She walked her fingers up and down his thigh. "I'm trying to solve the mystery as to how you have a pair of new jeans when you were with me practically all day and the stores in Shoshone aren't open on Sunday."

"Two words. Pam Mulholland."

"She bought these?"

"Plus two other pairs, and two more shirts. She gave them to me when I went to pick up my clothes. Too bad it was a wasted effort. She and Sarah thought it would be better if I had riding clothes so I could go out on horseback with Jack."

"Don't give up on that, Wyatt. Sarah is a powerful woman."

"I don't think even Sarah can bring Jack and me together. The gap is huge."

"How huge? You didn't tell me what was said."

"It wasn't pretty." The truck hit a rut and Wyatt wrestled with the wheel until the vehicle settled down again. "First he accused me of walking around like I owned the place."

"Ouch. That's harsh."

"Then he made it clear I wasn't a Chance and I'd better keep my mitts off his kid."

"I'm sorry, Wyatt. Didn't anyone come to your defense?"

"Josie tried but Jack was on his high horse, staking his claim to this land and letting me know I didn't belong here. So I told him to thank his lucky stars that my mother had left him here."

"Oh?"

"Yeah, I let him know that living with her had been its own kind of hell. I offered to compare situations any day of the week. Not long after that Jack ordered me off *his* land."

Olivia winced. She could see why the confrontation hadn't gone well, but she didn't think Wyatt would like what she had to say about it. He was convinced that dealing with his mother had been as bad or probably worse than being left at a tender age as Jack had been.

She was on Wyatt's side in this because he'd made the gesture toward friendship with his half brother. But that gesture would be worthless if he insisted that his life had been more miserable than Jack's. It wasn't a contest to prove who had suffered more.

But she chose not to say all that right now. They were heading up into the forest, Wyatt's favorite environment. Maybe when he was surrounded by nature he'd be able to open his mind to a new way of looking at his situation with Jack. If he stubbornly held to his current thinking, his cherished wish to unite with his half brother was doomed.

She hated that prospect for many reasons. It would mean Jack and Wyatt would miss out, but so would Sarah and the rest of the family. Wyatt was a warm and caring man, and he could enrich the family dynamics in so many ways.

But someone else would miss out, and that was her. Much as she wanted to believe Wyatt would consider settling in Shoshone whether his half brother approved or not, Olivia knew the reality. Jack's animosity, if it continued, would eventually kill Wyatt's urge to move his business here.

As for her, she was in Shoshone for the duration. It was her father's dream, and she wasn't planning to leave Grover Sedgewick to his own devices. Ever.

15

Wyatt drove until he spotted a trail going off to the left and up a hillside. He and Olivia didn't have much daylight left, so they needed to set up camp soon. Much as he hated to admit how right Sarah had been, leaving the ranch boundaries to find a camping spot wouldn't have worked. They'd started too late to be particular.

Fortunately he had plenty of experience in getting an expedition moving down the trail. After taking the time to switch out his borrowed cowboy boots for hiking boots, he quickly loaded most of the gear on his aluminum rack. Then he parceled out the rest for Olivia to carry in a small backpack. Locking the truck, he pocketed the keys and led the way up the trail.

Jeans weren't as comfortable for hiking as shorts, especially new jeans, but he relished the feel of the trail under his feet and the smell of pine and damp earth. He'd brought a fire starter that would help deal with wet kindling. A chill penetrated his cotton shirt, and he wanted a fire to keep them warm as well as to cook their food. He'd elected to leave the stove in the truck.

He called back periodically to check on Olivia,

but she insisted she was fine, so he pressed on. They crossed a couple of shallow streams, using flat rocks as stepping stones. After about forty-five minutes of hiking he found the kind of spot he was looking for. The pine needle-covered area was perfect for pitching the tent, and enough loose rocks lay around that he could construct a small fire pit.

"This will do," he said.

"Oh, thank God." Olivia sank down on a large rock and gulped for air.

"Olivia? Are you okay?" Slipping off his pack, he hurried over to her.

"Just a little…winded."

"You should have said something." He eased the pack from her and dropped it to the ground. "I thought you were fine back there."

"Well, I was, at first." She put a hand to her chest. "And then I kept thinking we'd stop any minute, so I didn't want to call a halt and look like a wimp."

"Aw, Olivia." He felt like a louse. He'd known that she wasn't used to this, but he'd been so focused on getting away from the beaten path that he'd accepted her assurances without turning around to really look at her. If he had he would have known she was struggling. "I'm so sorry."

"Doesn't matter." She gazed up at him. "We're here in our own private little world now, right?"

"That's what I was going for, and yeah, I think we're pretty much alone up here."

"But we need to do stuff before it gets dark." She started to stand.

"I'll do stuff." He placed a restraining hand on her

shoulder. "You watch. In fact, I'll bring you a glass of wine to sip on while I set things up."

"But you were going to teach me how to camp. How can I learn if I sit and drink wine while you do all the work?"

"It's not that complicated. Once you observe how it's done you'll be able to handle it yourself, no problem." He returned to his pack and started pulling things out. Eventually he unearthed the wine box and a couple of plastic glasses.

She laughed. "You're just trying to make me feel better."

"No, I'm actually trying to get you relaxed and tipsy so I can have my way with you inside the tent."

"I don't think you'll have to work quite so hard to achieve that outcome."

"Good to know." But he tapped into the wine box anyway, filled one of the glasses from the plastic spigot and brought it over. Then he crouched down in front of her. "Your suggestion of camping was a lifesaver. I wasn't sure what I was going to do once Jack and I had our confrontation, but this…this really helps."

"I'm glad."

"You've been such a bright spot in this whole crazy episode, Olivia." He looked into her eyes. "No matter what happens, I—"

"If you're preparing me for the fact that you're going back to San Francisco never to return, I don't want to hear it. Besides, I don't believe it. You really like Jackson Hole and you're not that committed to staying in San Francisco. I say screw Jack Chance and make your own plans."

He smiled. "I like your spirit."

"Fortunately that's not all you like." She winked at him and took a long swallow of her wine. "Ah. I think I'll live."

"Excellent news. Sit there while I show off my expertise." He stood and walked over to his pack. "We camping technicians love doing that, you know."

"Then I'll stroke your ego until you let me stroke something more interesting."

His cock twitched and he turned back to her. "On second thought, maybe we should forget about the tent and just sleep under the stars."

"No, thanks. This camping virgin wants to feel safe and cozy inside a zipped-tight tent."

"Fair enough. So allow me to present our room for the night." He unrolled it with a flourish. "Lightweight, but capable of providing shelter for...whatever you have in mind."

"Hmm. You've admitted you spend more time in the woods than in your apartment, and I know for a fact that you like sex, so if this tent could talk, it—"

"—it would say it is brand-new this season, barely used."

Olivia's gaze challenged his. "So are you saying that this tent has never experienced passion?"

Wyatt couldn't help laughing. "Sadly, it has not." Last year's hadn't seen any action, either. He'd have to go back to the tent before that before he could claim one with a sexual past. Or sleeping bags with a sexual past, come to think of it. These had been new last summer.

"Good." She drank more wine. "I like that."

He hid a smile. If she liked the idea of being the first

lover he'd had in this tent, she might be getting posses-sive, which would be a good sign. It was a short trip from feeling possessive to serious pursuit.

"First we get the poles in place…" He assembled them quickly and fit them into the pockets in the nylon. "And presto, the tent is gloriously erect."

She spewed her wine but fortunately it only went into the dirt and pine needles at her feet. "You said it like that on purpose."

"Maybe." He watched as she licked stray drops of wine from her mouth and his cock twitched again.

"What's next?"

"A couple of self-inflating air mattresses." He pulled the bungee cords off each one and opened the valves before crouching down and allowing them to unroll on the tent floor. One thing about new denim—it didn't have much give to it when a guy had a hard-on. He stood, grimacing.

She gazed at his crotch. "Something else seems to be inflating."

"Nice of you to notice."

"I know nothing about camping but it seems to me that once you put the sleeping bags on those rapidly in-flating air mattresses, which are übercool, by the way, you're in business."

"Well, the tent's ready, but I haven't constructed a fire pit or gathered wood or…" He had the good sense to stop listing chores as she drained the last of her wine, set down the glass and started untying her sneakers. He was even smart enough to grab the sleeping bags and unroll them on top of the air mattresses.

When he stood and turned back to her, he was

greeted by a sight that put the ultimate strain on the fly of his new jeans. She'd taken off both her T-shirt and her bra, and was in the process of unfastening her jeans.

He must have let out a little moan of need, because she glanced up. "Those jeans look uncomfortable," she said with a tiny smile. "Why don't you take them off?"

"Great suggestion." But before he did that he rummaged in his pack for the item he should have pulled out even before the wine. Tossing the box of condoms into the tent, he proceeded to get naked, but he was slower than Olivia. For someone who had never been camping, she sure did know how to occupy a tent in a hurry.

By the time he dropped to his knees to crawl in, she'd unzipped both sleeping bags and was nestled on the soft flannel interior like a centerfold.

He took a moment to admire her lying there. This tent would never look the same to him now. "I think you're getting the hang of this camping business," he murmured.

"I have a good teacher." Her gaze roamed over him in frank appreciation. "Coming in?"

"You know it."

"Don't forget to close that zipper thing. I like being close to nature, but I don't want nature to get too close, if you know what I mean."

"I hope that doesn't include me." He turned back once he was inside and zipped the flap.

"Actually, I was just thinking that I don't know you well enough."

"For what?" He glanced back at her, hoping to hell she wasn't about to shut down all his fantasies about having sex in this tent.

"I just think I need to get better acquainted with you if we're going to share a tent tonight."

"You want to talk...now?" He could barely contain his disappointment.

"I was imagining more of a hands-on learning experience."

"Oh." His disappointment evaporated in the heat of her gaze and his heart thudded heavily in anticipation of what she had in mind.

She patted the sleeping bag next to her. "Lie down on your back so I can get started."

He complied because only an idiot wouldn't follow directions like that. "Is this like when I used to play doctor with Mary Sue Jefferson in first grade?"

"Sort of." She cupped his face in one hand and feathered a kiss over his mouth. "Except I venture to say that I will do a better job than Mary Sue ever dreamed of doing."

As she began touching him, kissing him and generally rocking his world, he had to agree with that assessment. She became *very* well acquainted with all parts of his body, especially the part that had been standing at attention ever since she proposed this learning exercise. She licked and nibbled her way around that territory until he regretfully had to call a halt.

"But I have more to learn." She closed her mouth over the tip of his cock and sucked gently.

"Any second now you're going to learn that my control is shot." He gasped and clenched his jaw. "And then you'll learn how long it takes me to recover."

She lifted her head and met his gaze, but she kept her clever fingers wrapped around his johnson. "So I have to choose between making you come or allowing us both to come."

"That pretty well sums it up."

"Let me think about it." She ran her tongue over her lips as she slid her hand up and down in a motion guaranteed to produce results.

He grasped her wrist. "Much as I've loved this, and I have, I want to enjoy the entire experience, at least this time." He removed her hand from his cock and rolled to his side. "We can fool around with this program later, but…" rolling her to her back, he moved over her "…I want the whole enchilada, me and you, doing it the old-fashioned way."

Her blue eyes darkened and her breathing changed. "I could be talked into that."

"Good." Balancing on his forearm, he reached for the box of condoms. Dexterity proved valuable as he opened the box one-handed and pulled out a foil package.

"I'll take it from here." She plucked it from his grasp and ripped it open. "Now that I've mapped the territory."

"Just make it quick." He groaned at the brush of her fingers as she began the task. "I'm holding on by a thread." The snap of latex was music to his ears.

"That's it." She cupped his face and gazed up at him. "Bombs away."

That made him laugh, but it didn't stop him from burying himself up to the hilt. Laughing and thrusting made for an interesting combination, but soon the laughter faded as incredible friction claimed all his attention.

Holding his gaze, she arched upward, catching his rhythm and intensifying each stroke with movement of her own. Her lips parted and her breath came in tiny gasps, then whimpers, then cries of pleasure.

His breath hissed out as he felt her first spasm. "This is so good."

She moaned. "Yes."

He bore down, picked up the pace, felt his own climax hovering, reined it in. "I hope…we can…do it again…sometime."

She gulped for air. "Me, too. Oh, me, too!" She came then, his name a shout of joy on her lips.

Surrendering to the fierce pressure in his groin, he erupted with a groan of pure pleasure. As he lay there panting, careful not to collapse completely onto her, she sighed.

"Now the tent has known passion," she murmured.

"Yes." He drew a shaky breath. "It most certainly has."

WYATT DIDN'T GET THE FIRE built until after dark, but he was enough of a pro to accomplish it using a flashlight. Olivia was suitably impressed with his skills and told him so. This camping gig was turning out to be fun.

She'd felt quite daring when she'd exited the tent naked as a jaybird, as her father would say. She'd put her clothes back on, though, because once the sun had gone down the chill had set in. Knowing her hair was a mess after rolling around in the tent with Wyatt, she'd tied it back with the scrunchie she'd had the presence of mind to tuck in her pocket before leaving her purse in Wyatt's truck.

As they ate spaghetti and drank more wine, Olivia's thoughts went back to the reason they were here in the first place—Wyatt's problem with Jack. In some ways, it was none of her business. And yet, it was her business if the feud between the half brothers affected whether Wyatt would move his company to the Jackson Hole area or leave it in San Francisco.

If Wyatt moved to Shoshone, they had a future. If he stayed in California, they did not. She wasn't ready to commit to that future yet because she didn't want another failed engagement on her conscience. But she wouldn't mind having a fighting chance to create something lasting between them.

If she and Wyatt were ever going to be more than a fling, his attitude toward Jack had to be addressed before they returned to the ranch. She couldn't think of a better time than now, when they sat snuggled side by side on a ground cloth in front of the fire.

Wyatt had set their tin plates aside and wrapped his arm around her waist as they finished their wine. They'd made wonderful love an hour ago and she hoped they'd do it again soon.

But after another round of lovemaking she expected both of them to fall into an exhausted sleep. It had been an eventful couple of days. She'd sleep better knowing they'd talked this out.

Maybe he was already rethinking his stance. She hoped so, and she'd start from there. "Wyatt?"

He pulled her closer. "Ready for bed?" His voice was rich with promise.

"Not quite." She finished her wine and set her glass beside her. "I want to ask you something."

"Ask away."

"Now that some time has gone by, do you have any thoughts about Jack and the Last Chance?"

He tensed. "I'd rather not talk about Jack tonight, if you don't mind."

She gave a mental sigh. This wasn't going to be easy, after all. "I do mind. I...I have a stake in this now. I'd like you to move your business here, and I'm worried that after your fight with Jack you'll reconsider that."

He was quiet for a while, but he finally responded. "I won't lie to you, Olivia. Jack's behavior this afternoon makes me wonder if I'm just beating my head against a stone wall."

"I wouldn't look at it quite that way."

"No? I told you what he said."

"Yes, and you told me what you said." She chose her words carefully. "Obviously each of you has an ax to grind, but—"

"But what, Olivia? How can I expect to make progress with Jack when all he can think about is my connection to Diana, the woman he hates?"

"It's logical that he would. I'm sure he's still devastated that she abandoned him and chose to raise another family."

"But if only he could see that he got rid of a lousy mother and ended up with Sarah, who is wonderful. But no, he has the nerve to be upset with me, as if I had it better than he did because our mother stuck around while I was growing up."

Olivia was determined to hang on to her patience. "But if you could see it from his viewpoint, then maybe—"

"How about if he saw it from my viewpoint? If he had to spend even a week with Diana, he'd be a raving maniac. I guarantee it."

She said the words as gently as she knew how. "It's not a competition to prove who suffered more, Wyatt."

"I realize that, but her leaving him turned out to be for his own good." Wyatt's body had gone rigid with frustration. "Why can't he see that?"

She gazed into his angry eyes. "Does it really matter what he sees or doesn't see? Why not just acknowledge that he had a rough time and move on?"

"I wish it could be that simple, but I don't think it can. He couldn't even trust me to hold his kid, as if I'm permanently tainted because I'm Diana's son." His voice vibrated with pain.

"Give him another chance. I mean, when the stakes are this high, and you want to be part of this family—"

"Yeah, what a fantasy that was. To think I imagined blending into life on the ranch. I can kiss that idea goodbye."

"Maybe not. Wyatt, be the bigger man. Extend the olive branch to your brother."

"I've done that, and he slapped it out of my hand."

She stood up and faced him. "Could it be because you insisted on claiming that you were more damaged than he was?"

"Olivia, I made the trip from San Francisco. Twice. He wasn't particularly welcoming the first time, but I thought he'd get used to the idea, and I…I thought I'd finally found where I belonged."

"I know." She ached for him.

His jaw tightened. "But I can't keep laying everything on the line. It's time for Jack to step up."

"It's not a matter of stepping up." She began to wonder if she was wasting her breath. "It's a matter of wanting to heal this breach, of being willing to swallow your pride. Don't abandon the possibility of being part of that ranch community because you're too proud to try again."

He sighed and shook his head. "It's no use. I feel like the stray dog that keeps getting turned away. A man has to maintain some sense of dignity."

"But if you don't make peace with Jack then you and I have no future, because I'm here to stay. You do get that, right?"

He gazed at her, his expression unreadable. "Yes, and I'm sorry."

Which meant he wasn't going to try and work things out with Jack. As the reality of that sank in, a blanket of misery enveloped her. She'd watched him pull off one heroic deed after another, including spending time with her father and losing gracefully at chess.

She'd thought all he'd need was a nudge to be a hero in this instance, too. Instead he clung to his belief that he'd done all he could. He seemed willing to doom their relationship before it ever really blossomed.

16

ACCEPTING DEFEAT, OLIVIA helped Wyatt secure the camp for the night. They sacked the food and dishes together and used a rope to hang the bundle from a tree branch. Then they made sure the fire was totally out before they crawled into the tent, both of them fully dressed. Olivia put her shoes in the corner where she could find them easily.

"Let me get the flap." Wyatt started to zip it.

"That's okay. I might need to go out during the night."

"You're sure? I thought you were worried about critters."

"I'm more worried about desperately having to pee and not being able to find the tab on the zipper."

"Okay." He settled back on his sleeping bag.

They lay there in silence because there was nothing more to say. Although Olivia might have gotten some sleep, she felt as if she spent the whole night staring into the dark, waiting for the first light of dawn. She'd had such hopes for Wyatt, but if he put his pride ahead of all he had to gain by staying in Jackson Hole then he wasn't the man for her. Time to cut her losses and get away from him before he broke her heart permanently. It already felt slightly cracked.

After an eternity her surroundings became more visible. The sun wasn't up yet but it soon would be, and by then she wanted to be out of here. Wyatt slept soundly, his breathing rhythmic and undisturbed.

Her heart ached for him, and for Jack and their inability to see each other's point of view. But she'd given peacemaking a shot and Wyatt was more unwilling to bend than she'd realized. Maybe Sarah would be able to effect some change in the status quo, but Olivia wouldn't bet on it. Both men seemed as immovable as the granite rock marking the sacred site.

That rock was her destination now. Logic told her she wouldn't make it all the way back to the ranch before Wyatt woke up and missed her, even factoring in the time he'd take to break camp. She might not even have the stamina to walk all the way back. But she could make it to that rock and wait for him there.

Slipping out of the tent with her shoes, she shivered and zipped her hoodie. Then she sat down and put on her sneakers. Any distance she covered before Wyatt caught up with her would be that much less time she had to spend with him. After what they'd shared she couldn't bear the thought of packing up the camping supplies and enduring a hike with him back down the hillside.

But she needed to leave a note so he wouldn't panic. That was a challenge, but eventually she found a scrap of cardboard left over from the pasta box. A small piece of charred wood from the fire worked as a charcoal pencil.

"Headed down the trail. See you on the road or back at the ranch."

Moving as quietly as she could, she crept out of the camp and started down the trail. Every second she expected to hear Wyatt calling out to her, but he must have been really exhausted because the surrounding forest was silent in the gray light.

Once she was out of sight of the tent, she sighed and quickened her pace. She'd made it. Without a pack to weigh her down, she should reach the dirt road in no time. Her hair swung forward as she walked, and as she shoved it behind her ears, she realized that she'd lost the scrunchie sometime during the night. She sure as hell wasn't going back for it, though.

As she continued to walk the forest creatures began waking up. Birds chirped in the branches overhead and the underbrush rustled off to her left. A squirrel hopped out, bounded across the trail and scurried up a tree. Cute.

If Olivia were a heroine in a Disney movie she would break into song about now and the forest creatures would gather round and join in. Then Prince Charming would add his voice to the melody as he rode toward her on his gallant white horse. He'd scoop her into his arms and true love would be born.

Yeah, right. She could kiss that fairy tale goodbye. Apparently the guy who'd come to her rescue riding his gallant white truck hadn't read the script. It was all downhill from here. Ha.

She appreciated the ease of going down instead of up,

though. And when she caught a glimpse of three deer watching her through the trees, she stopped to admire them. The sight of the deer reminded her that there was a whole world out there that didn't revolve around her and her problems.

That made a very good case for getting out into nature on a regular basis, and she decided to do that. After all, she now lived in the middle of God's country. She could understand why Wyatt had chosen the profession he had, because seeing natural beauty on a constant basis could give a person perspective. Too bad he hadn't gained a little more of it.

Now that she'd challenged his assumptions he'd probably pack up his truck and leave the area for good. If she felt dismal knowing that would be the outcome, she'd have to get over it. Maybe she'd do that by taking more hikes. Obviously it wasn't that complicated, since she was doing fine all by herself this morning.

As she congratulated herself on her excellent plan to walk back to the road, showing some initiative and independence, she came to a fork in the trail. For one uneasy moment she stood there, undecided. The rocks and trees along each path looked about the same.

Finally she shrugged and chose the path on her left. Both of them headed downhill, and if she didn't come out right where the truck was parked, so what? All she needed to find was the road that would take her to the sacred site, and eventually, the ranch.

WYATT WOKE UP WITH A VAGUE feeling that something was wrong. He lay there with his eyes closed and quickly remembered why he'd feel that way. Olivia, who had seemed so supportive at first, had let him know last night she didn't approve of how he was handling things with Jack.

The tent was very quiet, so when he turned to find she wasn't lying next to him, he wasn't surprised. Her shoes were gone, but a neon-green bit of cloth lay on the sleeping bag and he picked it up. She'd put that in her hair last night after they'd had such great sex in here.

His gut twisted. He wished they'd had the kind of night he'd been hoping for, with a lot more sex and absolutely no discussion about Jack. And now…now he didn't know where they were. Nowhere, probably.

He didn't dare dwell on that thought too long or he'd discover just how into her he was. Technically they hadn't known each other long enough for him to be hooked on her. Then he thought about that kiss while they stood on the sacred site. He'd never had that kind of reaction to a woman before, where he'd had visions of a future with her flash before his eyes.

They should probably talk some more. He'd bet she could use a cup of coffee. Yeah, that was the way to go. Breakfast, coffee, the peaceful sounds of the forest first thing in the morning—that would bring them closer together.

Feeling more positive, he grabbed his hiking boots from the corner of the tent, stuck her hair doodad in his pocket and crawled out. A quick scan of the area as he sat down to put on his boots told him she wasn't there, but that didn't worry him. She'd probably found a private place to pee.

After he took care of that little matter himself, he walked back into camp expecting to see her. When she wasn't there, he called her name. No answer. He called again, louder this time. Still no answer.

For the first time since discovering she wasn't beside him in the tent, he became concerned. He searched the campsite more thoroughly and finally discovered the note she'd left on a scrap of cardboard. *Shit.* She had a head start but he was pretty damned fast when he needed to be.

Leaving everything except for his cell phone, he loped down the trail. A couple of times he paused to call out for her, but when there was no answer he wondered if she would even answer if she heard him. Maybe not. He kept going and made it to the truck in twenty minutes.

Still no sign of her. Her purse and cell phone were in the cab where she'd left them, but then they would be. She didn't have keys.

Fighting panic, he unlocked the truck and started it up. She wasn't in shape for a long walk, but adrenaline could make a difference. He drove back the way they'd come, constantly scanning the road for her.

When he reached the sacred site and still didn't see her, the cold sweat of anxiety trickled down his spine. This was not good. Not good at all.

And he wasn't going to waste any more time. He got out his cell and called the ranch, thinking he'd get either Mary Lou or Sarah. Instead he got—Murphy's Law—Jack.

He wasn't sure why Jack was answering the ranch phone early in the morning when he had his own house on the property where he lived with his wife and that baby he didn't want Wyatt touching. But no matter. This was an emergency and he had a feeling Jack was good at handling those, in spite of being stubborn as a mule.

"It's Wyatt," he said. "Is Olivia there?"

"Here? I thought she was with you."

"We had a…disagreement last night and I think she must have decided to walk back."

"I'll check." Jack was swearing as he got off the phone.

Sarah picked it up. "Wyatt? What's going on?"

"I think Olivia decided to walk back to the ranch."

"What on earth would have made her— Hold on. Jack's here." She came back in a second. "He says she's not in the house and her Cherokee is still parked where she left it. He's driving out there. Where should he meet you?"

"I'm at the sacred site, but I'm going back to the trailhead and make sure I didn't miss her somewhere between here and there. Tell Jack to keep going beyond the site about two miles and look for my truck. I'll stay there and wait for him."

"Got it. And, Wyatt?"

"Yeah?" He braced himself for whatever blame she might heap on his head.

"Don't worry, son. You two will find her."

"Thanks, Sarah." He wasn't used to quiet confidence in a mother figure. He was used to blame and panic. Rafe had done a disappearing act when they were about ten and Diana had been next to useless.

Yeah, he envied Jack having Sarah as a steadying influence most of his life, but Olivia's comments had stuck with him. He knew what total rejection felt like. He'd just experienced it from his half brother. How much worse would it be if it was your mother, and you were only two?

Turning the truck around, he started back down the road, going slower, checking the roadside in case she'd gone into the trees to rest or...no, he wouldn't start imagining all the terrible things that could happen to her alone out here. That wouldn't help.

No matter how thoroughly he searched both sides of the road as he crept back down the road, he saw nothing but rabbits, some quail, and back in the trees, a lone buck. What color had her blouse been? Oh, yeah, the same green as the scrunchie in his pocket. It was a color that could blend with the landscape, especially if she'd fallen down and... Once again he pulled his thoughts away from disaster.

Because the plain fact was he couldn't lose her. Not physically, and not emotionally either. She'd only tried to help last night, and he'd been a jerk who didn't realize what an incredible woman she was. She probably wanted to knock his and Jack's heads together, and he had to admit they deserved it.

But in order for her to do that, they had to find her. And by God, they would. He'd thought he never wanted to speak to Jack again, and here he was filled with relief and gratitude that his half brother was coming to the rescue.

OLIVIA HAD DONE SOME BONEHEAD things in her life, but this one had to be the worst. She'd hiked for well over an hour, although she couldn't be sure because she had no watch. And she had no idea where she was.

Instead of continuing down, the trail she'd chosen

ran along the side of the hillside. Once she realized her mistake, she'd turned around and started back only to find another fork she hadn't noticed before. Once again, she'd picked wrong.

She'd crossed a stream, thinking she was finally headed in the right direction because she remembered she and Wyatt had crossed two streams. The trail ended in a bluff that dropped thirty feet. She gazed out across the canopy of trees and searched in vain for the road. If it was there she couldn't see it from where she stood.

After wandering around on different trails, she'd finally had to admit that she was truly lost. And what did she, a girl from Pittsburgh, know about getting lost in the woods? Somewhere she'd read that you were supposed to signal searchers with something like a mirror or smoke.

She had no mirror and no matches. No doubt Wyatt had all that kind of stuff, but she'd elected, in her infinite wisdom, to set out on her own and leave her wilderness guide. But he was looking for her. She never doubted that for a second.

The only tool she had available was her voice, so she sat down on the bluff and started shouting for help. That lasted for about thirty seconds before her throat hurt. All she'd accomplished was putting a major scare into the little brown birds watching her from a nearby branch.

Besides, if Wyatt was searching, wouldn't he be calling for her? Therefore, if she couldn't hear him, he couldn't hear her. Then she remembered something else she'd heard about getting lost. Stay put and let the searchers come to you.

She could do that. She was dead tired, thirsty and hungry. If she sat here and listened for Wyatt calling her name, then she could respond when she heard him. Although she'd wanted to get as far away from him as possible this morning, she would be very glad to see him now.

She stretched out on the rock in the sunshine. With her head cradled on her arm, she closed her eyes. Just one short nap was all she needed. Then she'd be fresh and ready to respond to her rescuers. In seconds she dozed off.

WYATT PARKED THE TRUCK at the trailhead and got out. He wanted to start back up the trail to search some more, but he'd told Jack he'd wait for him. So he paced beside the truck and tried to estimate how long it would take Jack to get there.

No matter how long it took, waiting for Jack was the bright thing to do. Jack had grown up here and knew the trails, plus two searchers were better than one. If they didn't find her in the next couple of hours Wyatt was prepared to call in Search and Rescue.

But no need to get the authorities involved if it wasn't absolutely necessary. Wyatt knew instinctively that Jack would rather handle something like this internally if at all possible. Olivia hadn't been missing long…. *Missing*. What a stomach-turning, sweat-inducing concept. He wanted her back. In every sense of the word.

About two centuries went by before Wyatt saw a truck coming toward him. Because the road was still slightly muddy, the truck stirred up no dust. This time

Jack drove an ordinary ranch truck, which was a lot less imposing than the cherry-red semi.

When Jack parked the truck and climbed out, he looked every inch the cowboy in his Stetson, long-sleeved shirt and jeans. Every inch except for his feet. He had on deep-tread hiking boots.

Apparently he caught Wyatt staring. "You're not the only one allowed to wear them, you know."

"Yeah, but I didn't think—"

"That I'd tarnish my cowboy image?" Jack's dark eyes were neither hostile nor friendly. "My other boots are for riding and dancing, not for tramping through the forest." He walked around the front of the truck and opened the passenger door. "End of the line, pooch. Time to get to work."

No way. Wyatt came to the passenger side in time to watch Jack lift Rodney Dangerfield to the ground and snap a leash on the dog's collar. But the leash wasn't Rodney's only accessory. He was also wearing a bright orange life vest, a very snug life vest. The bottom of it scraped the ground.

"My God. He looks like…like…"

"A pig in a blanket? That's what I said, but Mom wanted him on the job and he has to wear his vest, even if it's a tad small, in case we hit water."

Rodney gazed up at Wyatt with his typical woebe-gone expression, which clearly said, "See what I have to put up with?" But his white-tipped tail wagged as if he'd accepted his lot.

Wyatt crouched down to scratch behind the dog's ears. "Thanks, Rod. Glad you're here."

"Now for the million-dollar question," Jack said. "Do you have anything of Olivia's we can give him to sniff?"

"Yeah, I do." Wyatt stood and fished in his pocket.

"I warn you, if you pull a pair of panties out of there I might have to deck you on general principles."

"You'd probably enjoy the excuse, but no such luck." He took out the green scrunchie. "She left this in the tent."

"Good. That should work. Got water? I forgot to bring any."

"Good thought. She'll be parched after hiking around all morning. Let me get my spare canteen." Wyatt sprinted back to his camper, grabbed the canteen and slung the strap over his shoulder.

"Okay, now let Rodney sniff that hair gizmo."

Wyatt hunkered down next to Rodney again. "Here you go, Rod. Find Olivia. Find her for us."

The basset made snuffling sounds as he inspected the scrunchie.

"That should do it," Jack said. "Okay, Rodney. Earn your keep."

17

WYATT STUFFED THE SCRUNCHIE back in his pocket in case they needed it later to refresh Rodney's memory. Nose to the ground, Rodney started toward the trail. That wasn't surprising. Olivia had walked that way yesterday afternoon.

As they started up the path, Wyatt decided to speak up. "I've never worked with a tracking dog before, but Olivia's scent could lead us to the camp because she walked up that way last night. But it will be a waste of time because she's not there now."

"I'm no expert, but I think he'll follow her old scent until he picks up something fresher." Jack allowed Rodney to lead the way. "At that stage we'll know we're tracking where she went more recently."

"Okay. That's logical." Concerns eased, Wyatt followed behind Jack. "Didn't expect you to answer the phone at the house this morning."

"That's because you don't know Sarah well enough yet."

"I don't get what you mean."

"Last night was supposed to be a party, and she

didn't want any more unpleasantness so she didn't deal with me then. I was called on the carpet first thing this morning, though."

Wyatt winced. "You know, Jack, I—"

"Save it. She's right. You're a guest in our home."

"Uninvited."

"Doesn't matter. Mom took you in, gave you a bed and showed you the best of Last Chance hospitality. I treated you like an intruder. I…had my reasons, all tied up with my kid and Diana, but…I regret how that all came down."

Wyatt could only imagine what it cost Jack to admit that he'd mishandled a situation. His chest tightened with empathy. "I regret the things I said, too, Jack. For the record, I got some similar behavior tips from Olivia. Thing is, I wasn't in a mood to hear them."

After another moment of silence, Jack blew out a breath. "When are we ever ready to hear shit like that?"

Wyatt smiled. "Good point. Speaking for myself, I can be a stubborn son of a bitch." He realized this kind of high-intensity conversation was best carried on exactly the way they were doing it, in the midst of a serious task, when they didn't have the opportunity to sit and look at each other.

"I've been called that a time or two," Jack said. They walked in silence for several minutes while Rodney kept his nose to the ground.

Wyatt wondered if that was the end of what they'd say on the subject. If so, that was okay. They'd made some progress.

But then Jack spoke again. "Sarah mentioned something this morning and I…" He took a deep breath. "I think she might be right about that, too."

"What's that?"

"She wondered if my rejection of you was payback, both to Diana, for rejecting me, and to you, because… because you didn't seem to understand how much…"

Wyatt wasn't going to make him say it. "I didn't," he said quietly. "But I do now. And it's partly because you rejected me, so in a way, you did me a favor there."

Jack's laugh was short. "Yeah, well, you won't get Sarah to agree with you."

"I might. Someday. That's assuming…" Now he was the one reluctant to say what he was thinking, in case he was wrong about where this exchange was heading.

"If you're wondering if you can hang around, the answer is yeah, I'd like that." Jack cleared his throat. "I'd like that a lot."

The tightness in Wyatt's chest loosened a little. Olivia was still out there and he wouldn't be able to relax until they found her, but knowing he and Jack were coming to an understanding gave him hope that they'd find Olivia, too. Between Wyatt's determination and Jack's knowledge of the area, they made a good team. Well, and Rodney, of course. Couldn't forget the basset hound and his excellent nose.

"Just one thing," Jack said.

"What's that?"

"Having you around—I'm okay with that. But having Diana show up is a whole other deal."

"Right." Wyatt felt the anxiety underlying Jack's statement.

"I'm doing my damnedest to separate you from her

in my mind," Jack continued. "I didn't do that very well last night, and when I saw you with Archie I had a sudden image of her holding him, and I...I really lost it."

Wyatt swallowed. "I understand. I won't let her become a problem." And he vowed that she wouldn't mess this up, for him, for Jack or for little Archie.

"Yeah? How are you going to keep her away?"

"Simple. Tell her she'll have to travel almost two hours' round-trip to get a decent latte. Issue handled."

Jack laughed. "Okay. That works."

It was the first time Wyatt had heard Jack laugh. He grinned to himself. Maybe he'd finally get to see the lighter side of Jack Chance.

OLIVIA WOKE TO LOUD BAYING of the kind she'd only heard in movies when they were tracking escaped convicts with bloodhounds. Rodney! Leaping up, she prayed that the baying was coming from the throat of a dog she knew and not from bloodhounds chasing an ax murderer through the woods.

She decided to take her chances. "I'm here!" She yelled as loud as she could, although her throat was dry from lack of water. "Over here!"

"Olivia!" Wyatt's voice had to be the sweetest sound in the universe.

"It's me!" She ran in the direction of the baying and Wyatt's voice. "You found me!"

Wyatt broke through the trees and they practically knocked each other down.

"Oh, my God." He held her tight, rocking her back and forth. "Oh, my God. You scared the crap out of me."

"I scared the crap out of myself." She hugged him

back just as hard. "But I knew you'd come. So I finally remembered if you're lost you're supposed to stay in one place, so I did." She heard Rodney yelping and whining, but she needed to keep holding on to Wyatt for just a little longer.

"Are you okay?" He pulled back to look at her. "Oh, I brought water." He lifted the strap over his head and unscrewed the cap.

"That's fabulous. I'm dying of thirst." She started to gulp it down.

"Go easy. Don't want you getting sick."

"Thanks." She made herself sip it.

"Sorry to interrupt, but this dog is going nuts trying to say hello."

That's when she finally realized Wyatt and Rodney weren't her only saviors. Jack Chance stood there holding a very taut leash. Rodney was ready to choke himself trying to reach her. And he was wearing…her hand went to her mouth to stifle a laugh. She shouldn't laugh at the dog who had so valiantly come to her rescue.

"Oh, Rodney." Handing the canteen to Wyatt, she went over to the dog and dropped to her knees so she could give him a proper hug. He slobbered all over her face and she didn't care. "You are the most handsome dog in the world, Rodney. When we get back I'm booking you an appointment for the works—shampoo, cut, blow-dry, nails, massage, you name it."

Rodney wiggled happily in her arms, whining as if to say he'd love that very much.

"It's his first official rescue," Jack said. "Guess I should give him the doggie treats I brought along."

"Definitely." Olivia stood and brushed off her jeans

as relief gave way to contrition. "Listen, you guys, I'm sorry to cause you all this trouble. Going off on my own like that was pretty dumb."

"Ah, it's just a rookie mistake." Wyatt sounded amazingly cheerful under the circumstances. "All's well that ends well."

"Yeah, it gave us a chance to test out the dog." Jack pulled two biscuits out of his pocket and tossed one to Rodney.

Rodney missed it, which both men seemed to find hilarious.

"Great tracker," Wyatt said. "But I wouldn't place any bets on him in a Frisbee tournament."

"You never know. With a little training..." Jack tossed the second biscuit in the air and Rodney missed that one, too.

Wyatt grinned at him. "The day you put Rodney in a Frisbee tournament is the day I dance *Swan Lake* in a tutu."

"You're on, twinkle toes. I already have it on good authority that you can shake your booty, so start practicing."

"Same to you, dog whisperer."

Olivia couldn't believe her ears. Somehow, some way, Jack and Wyatt had abandoned their hostility toward each other. Just like that. She didn't get it, but she wasn't going to question it either.

"Well, this has been fun," Jack said, "but some of us have work to do, so I'll be taking this Frisbee-champ-in-training back to my truck and heading for the ranch. Olivia, you can come with me or help our future ballerina pack up his gear. Up to you."

Olivia looked at Wyatt. "You left everything at the campsite?"

"Well, *yeah*."

"Oh."

"You thought I'd take the time to break camp when I knew you were somewhere out here by yourself?"

She saw the depth of concern in his eyes and knew she hadn't given him nearly enough credit. "I really screwed up, Wyatt. I'm so sorry."

His expression softened. "It's okay. I understand why you wanted to head out. Listen, you're probably exhausted. Don't worry about the camping gear. I'll bring it back down."

"No, I'm going to help you."

"Really, you don't have to—"

"I'm going to help you, damn it! It's the least I can do for someone I scared the crap out of, don't you think?"

Jack laughed. "She wants to help you, man. Take it from a guy who wasn't always smart about these things. Stop arguing with the lady and go with the flow."

Wyatt looked as if he wanted to say something else, but then he scrubbed a hand over his face. "All right. I'll take that advice."

"Good. See you two back at the ranch, then. Oh, and I'll take care of calling Mom to let her know Olivia's safe and sound."

"Thanks, Jack." Wyatt held out his hand.

"You're welcome…bro." Jack clasped his hand and the two men exchanged a long look.

Olivia had thought this day might never come, and yet it all seemed so easy now. Funny how quickly things could change sometimes.

Jack and Rodney took off and Olivia stood gazing at Wyatt. "That's amazing," she said.

"Yeah." Wyatt gave her a wry smile. "All it took was a couple of smart women to straighten out a couple of dumb guys." He stepped closer but didn't touch her. "Thanks for talking turkey to me last night. It took some time for it to filter through my thick skull, but of course you were right, about everything."

"I don't care who's right and who's wrong. I'm just happy that you and your brother are going to be friends."

"Me too." He hesitated. "What about us? Are we going to be friends?"

"I think there's a very good chance we are."

He looked down at the ground for a couple of seconds and cleared his throat. When his gaze met hers, it was completely unguarded and filled with passion and longing. "That's not good enough," he said.

"No?" Her heart began to pound.

"No." He reached for her, drawing her into his arms. "I want to be your friend, but I want much more than that. I want to be your lover."

She looked into his eyes. "The job's yours. You're very good at—"

"But I want more than that."

"You want to clean my house? Wyatt, I don't know what to say. I've always dreamed of—"

"Smart-ass." He pulled her in close. "I want to be the guy."

"The guy?"

"Yeah. The one you count on. I want to be the one you come to when something terrible happens and you're overwhelmed with grief. I want to be the one you race to when something great happens and you're filled with joy. I want to be there for you, Olivia."

Happiness hummed through her as she wrapped her arms around him and hung on, loving the solid warmth of his body. "Sounds like you're getting serious."

"Yeah." He smiled. "I am. Think you could be getting serious, too?"

She nodded.

"That's good news."

"But about cleaning my house. I really could use someone to—"

"I'll clean your damned house." His mouth hovered over hers. "I'll do whatever it takes if you'll let me love you."

"I think that can be arranged if the agreement goes both ways."

"Meaning?" His mouth brushed hers.

"If I let you love me, you let me love you."

"Lady, you have a deal." His mouth found hers, and she could swear the woodland creatures began to sing, just like in a Disney movie.

Epilogue

"So THERE YOU HAVE IT." Sarah picked up her mug of coffee and took a sip. "Wyatt has to lead a few wilderness expeditions, but in his spare time he'll be taking the necessary steps to transfer his business to Shoshone."

Sitting across from her at the kitchen table, Mary Lou nodded. "I think that's great. And his mother still doesn't know about little Archie?"

"Wyatt's not planning to volunteer the information, but I feel guilty every time I think about it. I'm wondering if maybe I should contact her and—"

"Don't buy trouble, Sarah. She hasn't exactly inquired about whether her son married and had a child, now, has she?"

"No, she hasn't." Sarah cradled her coffee mug. "That's a valid point. And she may end up here even without me contacting her. I fully expect Wyatt and Olivia to get married before the summer's out. They're so in love. I can't imagine Wyatt marrying Olivia without his family here, can you?"

"No, I can't. But do you think Jack sees all that coming down the pike?"

Sarah nodded. "I think he knew from the first time Wyatt showed up that it was only a matter of time before he had to confront his mother."

"His biological mother. You're his real mother."

"I appreciate you saying that, Mary Lou, but...he'll never be totally free of her, so maybe it's better if he faces her and gets it over with. If Wyatt and Olivia get married soon, as I predict, it will force the issue. That could be intense, but a good thing in the end."

"Guess so." Mary Lou pushed back her chair. "More coffee?"

"No, I should get busy. Pete's coming by in an hour to go over last-minute details for when the teenagers arrive."

"About that."

Something in Mary Lou's voice alerted Sarah. "Are you having second thoughts? I hope not, because they'll show up in a week and a half."

"I know." Mary Lou fiddled with her mug. "The thing is, Watkins finally wore me down."

"Wore you down?" Then Sarah's eyes widened. "You're getting *married?*"

Mary Lou actually blushed. "Stupid, isn't it?"

"No! It's wonderful! But we don't have much time to plan with the kids coming, but don't worry about that. We'll figure something out. Mary Lou, I'm so excited for you!" She hurried over to give her friend a fierce hug.

"No planning needed," Mary Lou said. "We're going on a twenty-one-day cruise starting next week, and we'll have the captain marry us on board the ship. It seemed like an easy solution and wouldn't cause anybody any trouble."

Sarah looked at her old friend in shock. "A cruise? So how long have you been planning this?"

"Not long. You know Tyler still has connections, and she arranged it all." Mary Lou's brow furrowed. "You're not upset, are you?"

"Of course not! It's just a surprise, that's all. A good surprise, but still. And I feel horrible asking this, because your happiness is more important, but what are we going to do about the meals while you're gone?"

"Oh, that's covered. I've asked my niece from Nebraska to come and fill in. Her name's Aurelia Smith, and she's a whiz in the kitchen. She'll be great."

"I'm sure she will be." Sarah took a deep breath and walked back to her chair. "Maybe I'll have a little more coffee after all." This was shaping up to be a morning that required extra caffeine.

As she was taking her first sip, her son Gabe burst into the kitchen. "Houdini's broken out of his stall for the last time. I say we sell that worthless piece of horseflesh."

"Good morning, Gabe." Sarah smiled at her youngest son. "Won't you have some coffee?"

Gabe blew out a breath that ruffled his mustache, a bit of facial hair he loved and his wife, Morgan, was less fond of. "Sure. Sorry, Mom. I've just had it with that horse." He poured himself coffee and came to join them at the table. "I know he's valuable and could be a good stud for us, but he's such a pain in the rear."

"Pete was talking about a trainer who seems to have

a way with horses like Houdini. His name's Matthew Tredway. Ever hear of him?"

"Well, yeah, who hasn't? But he's hard to get. And expensive."

"Pete seems to think he could get him. And Pete's willing to pay the up-front costs because he's convinced Houdini will earn it back later. I just need to clear it with you and your brothers before I give Pete the okay."

"Hey, tell Pete to go for it, Mom. I don't see a downside. I can't imagine Jack or Nick will, either. That horse is getting on everyone's last nerve."

"All right, then." Sarah took another bracing sip of her coffee. People were always coming and going on the Last Chance, and she wouldn't have it any other way. It kept her young.

* * * * *

There are more SONS OF CHANCE *on the way!*
Look for LEAD ME HOME,
available next month
wherever Harlequin books are sold.

PASSION

COMING NEXT MONTH
AVAILABLE JUNE 26, 2012

#693 LEAD ME HOME
Sons of Chance
Vicki Lewis Thompson

Matthew Tredway has made a name for himself as a world-class horse trainer. Only, after one night with Aurelia Smith, he's the one being led around by the nose....

#694 THE GUY MOST LIKELY TO...
A Blazing Hot Summer Read
Leslie Kelly, Janelle Denison and Julie Leto

Every school has one. That special guy, the one every girl had to have or they'd just die! Did you ever wonder what happened to him? Come back to school with three of Blaze's bestselling authors and find out how great the nights are after the glory days are over....

#695 TALL, DARK & RECKLESS
Heather MacAllister

After interviewing a thousand men, dating coach Piper Scott knows handsome daredevil foreign journalist Mark Banning is definitely not her type—but what if he's her perfect man?

#696 NO HOLDS BARRED
Forbidden Fantasies
Cara Summers

Defense attorney Piper MacPherson is being threatened by a stalker and protected by FBI profiler Duncan Sutherland. Her problem? She's not sure which is more dangerous....

#697 BREATHLESS ON THE BEACH
Flirting with Justice
Wendy Etherington

When PR exec Victoria Holmes attends a client's beach-house party, she has no idea there'll be cowboys—well, one cowboy. Lucky for Victoria, Jarred McKenna's not afraid to get a little wet....

#698 NO GOING BACK
Uniformly Hot!
Karen Foley

Army Special Ops commando Chase Rawlins has been trained to handle anything. Only, little does he guess how much he'll enjoy "handling" sexy publicist Kate Fitzgerald!

You can find more information on upcoming Harlequin® titles, free excerpts and more at www.Harlequin.com.

HBCNM0612

REQUEST YOUR FREE BOOKS!
2 FREE NOVELS PLUS 2 FREE GIFTS!

red-hot reads!

YES! Please send me 2 FREE Harlequin® Blaze™ novels and my 2 FREE gifts (gifts are worth about $10). After receiving them, if I don't wish to receive any more books, I can return the shipping statement marked "cancel." If I don't cancel, I will receive 6 brand-new novels every month and be billed just $4.49 per book in the U.S. or $4.96 per book in Canada. That's a saving of at least 14% off the cover price. It's quite a bargain. Shipping and handling is just 50¢ per book in the U.S. and 75¢ per book in Canada.* I understand that accepting the 2 free books and gifts places me under no obligation to buy anything. I can always return a shipment and cancel at any time. Even if I never buy another book, the two free books and gifts are mine to keep forever.

151/351 HDN FEQE

Name _____ (PLEASE PRINT)

Address _____ Apt. #

City _____ State/Prov. _____ Zip/Postal Code

Signature (if under 18, a parent or guardian must sign)

Mail to the **Reader Service:**
IN U.S.A.: P.O. Box 1867, Buffalo, NY 14240-1867
IN CANADA: P.O. Box 609, Fort Erie, Ontario L2A 5X3

Not valid for current subscribers to Harlequin Blaze books.

Want to try two free books from another line?
Call 1-800-873-8635 or visit www.ReaderService.com.

* Terms and prices subject to change without notice. Prices do not include applicable taxes. Sales tax applicable in N.Y. Canadian residents will be charged applicable taxes. Offer not valid in Quebec. This offer is limited to one order per household. All orders subject to credit approval. Credit or debit balances in a customer's account(s) may be offset by any other outstanding balance owed by or to the customer. Please allow 4 to 6 weeks for delivery. Offer available while quantities last.

Your Privacy—The Reader Service is committed to protecting your privacy. Our Privacy Policy is available online at www.ReaderService.com or upon request from the Reader Service.

We make a portion of our mailing list available to reputable third parties that offer products we believe may interest you. If you prefer that we not exchange your name with third parties, or if you wish to clarify or modify your communication preferences, please visit us at www.ReaderService.com/consumerschoice or write to us at Reader Service Preference Service, P.O. Box 9062, Buffalo, NY 14269. Include your complete name and address.

HBI1B

NEW YORK TIMES BESTSELLING AUTHOR
KAT MARTIN

Millions of lives are on the line. But for him, only one matters.

It's not in bodyguard Jake Cantrell's job description to share his suspicions with his assignments. Beautiful executive Sage Dumont may be in charge, but Jake's not on her payroll. As a former special forces marine, Jake trusts his gut, and it's telling him there's something off about a shipment arriving at Marine Drilling International.

A savvy businesswoman, Sage knows better than to take some hired gun's "hunch." And yet she is learning not to underestimate Jake. Determined to prove him wrong, Sage does some digging of her own and turns up deadly details she was never meant to see.

Drawn into a terrifying web of lies and deceit—and into feelings they can't afford to explore—Jake and Sage uncover something that may be frighteningly worse than they ever imagined.

AGAINST THE SUN

**AVAILABLE NOW
WHEREVER BOOKS ARE SOLD.**

New York Times *and* USA TODAY *bestselling author Vicki Lewis Thompson returns with yet another irresistible cowpoke! Meet Mathew Tredway—cowboy, horse whisperer and honorary Son of Chance.*

Read on for a sneak peek from the bestselling miniseries SONS OF CHANCE:

LEAD ME HOME Available July 2012 only from Harlequin® Blaze™.

As MATTHEW RETURNED to the corral and Houdini, the taste of Aurelia's mouth was on his lips and her scent clung to his clothes. He'd briefly satisfied the craving growing within him, and like a light snack before a meal, it would have to do.

When he'd first walked into the kitchen, his mind had been occupied with the challenge of training Houdini. He'd thought his concentration would hold long enough to get some carrots, ask about the corn bread and leave before succumbing to Aurelia's appeal. He'd miscalculated. Within a very short time, desire had claimed every brain cell.

Although seducing her this morning was out of the question, his libido had demanded some sort of satisfaction. He'd tried to deny that urge and had nearly made it out of the house. Apparently his willpower was no match for the temptation of Aurelia's mouth, though, and he'd turned around.

If he'd ever felt this kind of desperate need for a woman, he couldn't recall it. During the night, as he'd lain in his narrow bunk listening to the cowhands snore, he'd searched for an explanation as to why Aurelia affected him this way.

Sometime in the early-morning hours he'd come up with

the answer. After years of dating women who were rolling stones like he was, he'd developed an itch for a hearth-and-home kind of woman. Aurelia, with her cooking skills and voluptuous body, could give him that.

With luck, once he'd scratched this particular itch, he'd be fine again. He certainly hoped so, because he had no intention of giving up his career, and travel was a built-in requirement. Plus he liked to travel and had no real desire to stay in one spot and become domesticated.

Tonight he'd say all that to Aurelia, because he didn't want her going into this with any illusions about permanence. He figured that when the right guy came along, she'd get married and have kids.

Too bad that guy wouldn't be him....

Will Aurelia be the one to corral this cowboy for good?
Find out in: LEAD ME HOME

Available July 2012
wherever Harlequin® Blaze™ books are sold.

This summer, celebrate everything Western
with Harlequin® Books!
www.Harlequin.com/Western
